I0650399

Edith Neville

Alice Ashland

A romance of the World's Fair

Edith Neville

Alice Ashland
A romance of the World's Fair

ISBN/EAN: 9783337344993

Printed in Europe, USA, Canada, Australia, Japan

Cover: Foto ©Andreas Hilbeck / pixelio.de

More available books at **www.hansebooks.com**

ALICE ASHLAND

A ROMANCE OF THE WORLD'S FAIR

BY

EDITH NEVILLE

Specially written for " Once a Week Library"

NEW YORK
PETER FENELON COLLIER
1893

ALICE ASHLAND.

CHAPTER I

THE GREAT WHITE CITY which had sprung into existence, as if by the touch of a magician's wand, on the southwest shore of Lake Michigan, and known the wide world over as the "World's Fair," built in honor of the four hundredth anniversary of the discovery of America by that great navigator, Christopher Columbus, had been opened, as the go-ahead people of Chicago said it would be, on the first day of May, 1893. President Cleveland had touched the button, made his speech and departed. The Duke and Duchess of Veragua, representative of Columbus at the greatest show on earth, had been wined and dined ; and Eulalie, Infanta of Spain, had been initiated into the mysteries of Western society, and the woolly West had seen for the first time a real, live princess and was satisfied. The great and distinguished visitors had gone, and the Fair was left in possession of the hundreds of thousands who had journeyed

3

over land and sea to see the mighty collection
of exhibits, and representatives of every country under the sun were doing homage to Chicago.

The opening scene in our story does not com-
mence, however, at the Fair itself, but at one
of the fashionable racecourses of Chicago
known as the "Hawthorne" track, partly
owned and managed by that prince of sport,
Edward Corrigan, better known in the Windy
City as "The Master of Hawthorne." Thousands of visitors to the Fair, tired of the vain
attempt to see everything it contained, occasionally took a day off and visited some other
interesting spot in or around Chicago. On the
afternoon of the day on which our story begins
several thousand visitors and permanent Chi-
cagoans had journeyed to Hawthorne to witness the contests of thoroughbreds, and the
scene was one not easily forgotten — the grand
stand literally packed with ladies and gentlemen gayly attired, and the grounds swarming
with a mass of struggling humanity, at this
particular moment straining every nerve to
catch a glimpse of the favorite as he flies past
in the preliminary canter. The last bugle has
sounded, all the horses are at the post, and
after two or three breakaways there is a wild
yell of " They're off !" as the horses dash away

to a magnificent start, and the great and last race of the day had begun.

"I tell you, Mary," said a gentleman in the grand stand, to a lady by his side, "I tell you if Gendarme doesn't win I'll be stone broke."

"More fool you," replied the lady, keeping her glasses on the flying steeds.

The horses sweep past the grand stand, stretching across the track from rail to rail, almost in a perfect line, but the favorite Gendarme soon drops back, and Sterling, an eight-to-one shot, rushes to the front. As they swing round the first turn a quickening of pace and a change of position shows the favorite creeping up, and wild yells of "Gendarme!" are heard on every side. Rosemont and Minnie Beach have fallen back, and before they are half-way up the back stretch the others are hopelessly beaten.

Platoni, with his merciless whip and spurs, has driven Gendarme close to the flying leader. Every moment the pace is quickening, and a yell announces that the favorite has passed the outsider.

"That saves me!" ejaculates the young man in the grand stand.

"Not yet, Wilfred. Sterling is catching him." A cry from the enormous crowd bore out the lady's words. "Look at Gendarme!"

The great horse has fallen back so swiftly that before his startled backers can echo the cry he has been passed by Rosemont and Gold. The leaders are fully ten lengths away before Plantoni once more rallies the great horse and sets out in pursuit. They are now in the last one hundred yards of the race. Sterling has again assumed the lead, but Rosemont is at his saddle-girths and the favorite three lengths away, seeming to catch the leaders at every stride. The excitement has become intense. Friends of the favorite are shrieking encouragement to his jockey. Women are waving handkerchiefs hysterically. The air is full of cries. A few more strides and Gendarme is at Rosemont's side; wild and wilder grow the yells of "Gendarme wins! Gendarme wins!" and now the gallant animal is neck and neck with the leader, whose jockey has been sitting throughout the race almost motionless in the saddle; now he is seen to lean slightly forward and bring his whip across Sterling's flank, and that noble horse, responding gamely to the call, springs away from the favorite and with astounding ease canters in a winner by a full length. Gendarme, after one of the greatest races ever run at Hawthorne, finished second by a head from Rosemont; the rest were nowhere.

The result was too surprising to be applauded; it required a minute or two before the astonished crowd could catch its breath. Then the winner was heartily and enthusiastically cheered.

"Well, Mr. Nevin, I'm sorry you lost," said a slight, elegant woman by the side of the gentleman in the grand stand, who was, at the opening of the race, so interested in the favorite; "but hand me my wrap; Mary, let us be going. What is she looking at, Mr. Nevin?"

The lady addressed had been for a minute or so gazing through her race-glass at some person or persons standing near the judge's box, and now, turning to Nevin, she handed the glass to him.

"I wish," she said, "you would look at that man who is leaning against the fence with the brown straw hat on. I really believe it is Harold Neale."

"I daresay it is. He is in Chicago, I know," taking the glass and looking as she directed.

"Yes," he said, "it is Neale; you have a good memory, Mary."

"It is a long time since I saw Harold Neale, and he is a good deal changed. Why did you not bring him to see me?"

"I never thought of it," said Nevin.

"Well, go to him now, like a good boy, and invite him to supper."

Nevin raised his eyebrows, put on an air of submission and left the seat.

"You have a very obedient brother, Mary," said the first speaker.

"Yes, Mrs. Wainwright," returned the lady addressed, "every one obeys me."

"Except Major Craven," cried Mrs. Wainwright.

"That, of course. I promised to obey him," said Mrs. Craven, a smile parting her ripe red lips and showing the white, regular teeth within. She was a handsome likeness of her brother, Wilfred Nevin, with more vitality.

"Come!" resumed Mrs. Craven, "let us go. Mr. Stetson" (to a gentleman by her side who had been too interested in the racing to talk), "you can find the carriage, and Wilfred must come on the best way he can; I do hope he brings Harold Neale."

Mr. Stetson was most active and energetic, and the carriage was quickly brought up, and the owner, with her fair friend, carefully handed in by the devoted Stetson.

"I shall be at home to-morrow; come and have a cup of tea. Good-by," said Mrs. Craven, as the carriage rolled off.

"What a shame not to ask the poor fellow to

supper!" said Mrs. Wainwright. "He really earns his bread (his bread of life) very hardly."

"Nonsense!" returned Mrs. Craven; "four are company, five an unpleasant solitude; besides, I have given him his guerdon; tea with us is payment in full. I do not want him to-night."

"Oh, it is to be a double tete-a-tete? As you like. But who is this mysterious Harold Neale?"

"Harold Neale," said Mrs. Craven, slowly, "is the son of some people who occupy a farm close to ours, at Peekskill-on-the-Hudson. He was my first—well, nearly my love."

"Your first love! and you remember him! This is interesting."

"I assure you he was very interesting, and so desperately in earnest. He was ready to brave the wrath of all the Nevins if I would only run away with him. I answered him by marrying Major Craven."

"A very wise solution. What a nuisance it is, Mary, that nice men never have any money!"

"Well, rarely; but the Neales are fairly well off," responded Mrs. Craven, with a sigh.

"And where has your young hero been hiding himself?"

"I don't know. He was a medical student in

Philadelphia, but he broke away and went West
to Dakota or Puget Sound ; in short, he was in
disgrace with every one, so we quite lost sight
of him."

"Ah! I suppose remorse for having ruined
his life presses on your soul."

"Indeed it does not ; but he was a delightful
lover."

"I feel curious to see this hero," said Mrs.
Wainwright, yawning. "What are we to have
for supper ? I'm hungry."

"I scarcely know. The usual sort of thing,
I suppose."

"My dear, with your means you should aim
at uncommon things."

A little more disjointed talk brought them to
a residence in Evanston that Major Craven had
rented for the World's Fair season.

"I find it rather warm," said Mrs. Craven,
as they entered the house. Then taking a
silver matchbox from the mantelpiece and
lighting the candles in the girandoles at each
side of the glass, she looked steadily at her own
image for a minute, and then turned away with
a slight smile.

"You think you'll do ? " asked Mrs. Wainwright, who had been watching her lazily. "Is
the young man from the Hudson to be immo-
lated over again ? ".

Mrs. Craven laughed—a pleasant, joyous laugh.

"Certainly not; but I am glad my old admirer will not be able to say: 'Poor Mary is awfully gone off. Six or seven years are something of a trial to the best complexion, added to late hours and a rapid rate of living.'"

"Too true!" cried Mrs. Wainwright. "You make me shiver. Here am I, a destitute widow for more than three years, and I have only enjoyed, not improved, the shining hour. I really must find—"

"I hear a hack or something stop," interrupted Mrs. Craven, quickly. "Come, let us not seem to have waited for them."

But she had not yet taken her seat when "Mr. Nevin and Mr. Neale" were announced, and she went forward to greet her early lover.

"After long years!" she said, holding out her hand, with a soft smile. "I am very glad to see you, Mr. Neale."

Harold Neale was tall, broad and largely built. He was dark, either naturally or from exposure, with nearly black hair and deep gray steady eyes; there was a certain dignity of strength in his figure and movements which also gave him the air of being taller than he really was.

"You are very good to give me this pleasure," replied Neale, holding her hand for just a second. "I was most agreeably surprised when Wilfred brought me your invitation."

"Which I could hardly persuade him to accept," said Nevin; "and, ladies, we had quite an adventure on the road back."

"What was it? let's hear!" cried Mrs. Wainwright, excitedly.

"Well, while Harold and myself were waiting for a coupe there was a commotion among the crowd, and every one began to scatter like mice out of a stack, and along the road came a horse and buggy tearing like mad, an old gentleman and a young woman were clinging panic-stricken to the seat, powerless to grasp the reins which trailed on the road. Seeing that a collision would probably mean instant death, I sprang into the road, and just as the maddened animal, made madder still by the crowd, was dashing past I fortunately grabbed the reins, and after a severe struggle finally succeeded in stopping him; the young lady was in a dead faint, but the old gent thanked me heartily and insisted on having my card."

"How very interesting," cried Mrs. Wainwright, "but it seems to have upset your nerves, or you would introduce me to your friend; your sister seems to have forgotten my existence."

"You must forgive me," said Mrs. Craven. "Let me introduce my old friend and playfellow to you, Mrs. Wainwright. Mr. Neale, Mrs. Wainwright."

The well-assorted party sat down to dinner.

"How is Major Craven?" asked Harold Neale, after draining a glass of wine.

"He is quite well, I hope. Perhaps you think I ought not to have a supper party without him. Pray remember it is a family affair I have my brother's august protection, and you"—turning her soft eyes full on his—"almost belong to us. My husband is in New York; he is always going to and fro. I hope to introduce you to him on his return."

"Thank you. I shall not stay much longer in Chicago."

"Oh, you must not run away so soon; really the Fair is very delightful."

And thus conversing on the past and speculating on the future, the quartette contrived to pass a merry evening.

CHAPTER II.

HAROLD NEALE was busy writing letters about two weeks after the events of the preceding chapter, and had laid down his pen before answering an invitation to dinner from Major and Mrs. Craven for the following Friday.

"I suppose I must accept," he said to himself. "I have refused a musical evening and a party at Wilson's. I should like to see Mary's husband. It is a droll idea to meet him, too, without any deadly intentions. Come in," interrupting himself as some one knocked at the door.

"A gentleman wants to know if you'll see him, sir," said a waiter, presenting a card which bore the name of "Wilfred Nevin."

"Yes; show him up." And in a few minutes Wilfred walked in.

"I was just thinking of looking you up," cried Neale, shaking hands with him. "I have not seen anything of you since we supped together at Mrs. Craven's. I thought you would have come with me to the 'Home Rule' meeting to—"

"Bah! I have been otherwise engaged," interrupted Nevin, with some solemnity, as he drew a chair opposite his friend.

Neale looked at him, half amused at the mingled expression of triumph and uneasiness in his eyes.

"I have been very seriously occupied," repeated Nevin.

"What have you been about?"

"I have been securing a wife. I have been finding the means of living."

"What do you mean?"

"You remember that accident?"

"Yes."

"Well, the old gentleman who was driving the girl that day was her guardian, and you may well be astonished when I tell you that he instituted inquiries about their savior. Having determined that my pedigree was O. K., he wrote, inviting me to call. I called, and after thanking me effusively for my gallant conduct in stopping the runaways, he coolly told me that the young lady was 'for sale'; to be plain about it, she is an orphan, the niece of a California millionaire, and her two guardians, of whom the pompous old gent is one, have been looking for a suitable husband for the girl so as to get rid of her, and the trouble she and her legacy give them. Guardian No. 1 is satisfied with me, and Guardian No. 2 received me yes-

terday, and we got on very well, and it is agreed
I am to be officially introduced to the young
lady to-morrow."

"But you are not in earnest? You would
not select a wife in this fashion?"

"Why not? What is worse in it than being
introduced by — say my sister — to an heiress
with a view to matrimony? It is the same sort
of operation more openly and satisfactorily conducted. I, too, have been looking into matters,
and it is a bona fide ready money affair. In
short, I am inclined to think my luck has
turned."

"And the young lady?"

Nevin made a grimace. "I haven't seen her
since the accident, and as she fainted, she won't
remember me, and I'm sure I wouldn't know
her. I only hope she's not too utterly utter. If
she is, why I'll cry off. But, Harold, she has
close on two hundred thousand a year. *That*
will cover a host of defects. Then there are
many compensations for the most devoted husband, and I intend to be a model. She shall
spend a fair share of her own money as she
likes, while I shall amuse myself my own way—
in moderation."

"You are old enough to take care of yourself," said Neale ; "I confess I feel most for

the girl. I suppose she knows nothing about this precious scheme?"

"Hasn't the faintest suspicion. She will be enchanted with me, *if* I choose ; I always get on with women, and Miss Ashland (her name is Ashland) has been secluded all her sixteen years. Since the father's death my future spouse has lived in the paternal cottage, under the care of No. 2 guardian's sister, and I presume her manners wouldn't suit Ward McAllister. I have got Craven's lawyer to look into the matter, and he, too, says it is a bona fide concern."

There was a moment's silence.

"Why don't you congratulate me, Harold?"

"Perhaps I may later on ; at present—well, I don't like the scheme. But I suppose I take things too seriously. I daresay a marriage of this kind is no worse than a large proportion of those which occur every day."

"On the contrary, it is a great deal better—less nonsense and more reality. You are quite too desperately in earnest—always were, so Mary says. By the way, she is quite taken up with my plans. Will you come with me and support me in this crisis of my fate?"

"Where?"

"At the Fair to-morrow, in the French :

gallery, at 2 P.M., to meet the object of my adoration. She and Mr. Watts, the superior guardian, will be there. Really it will be fun for you to see the meeting."

" I will come," said Neale, slowly. "Where shall I find you?"

"Oh, pick me up at the Auditorium. We'll have a glass of sherry to keep up our spirits. You see, if the thing can be managed it will be a great chance for me. I am pretty well at my wit's end. Indeed, I must raise funds to carry out this scheme. Do you happen to have a few hundreds, Neale, you would like to lend at high interest?"

"Certainly not," with a grim smile. "I like you too much, old fellow, to have any transactions of that sort with you."

"Niggard!" cried Nevin, in mock heroic tones. "Well, I must sell one of my horses. In short, the only chance left me is this marriage. If it fails—but it must not fail. Now I have to escort Mrs. Wainwright to a garden party at Englewood. So good-by till to-morrow. Mind you don't fail me. You'll make a respectable sort of sponsor." With a nod he left the room.

Neale looked after his old playfellow with something of uneasiness as he thought, "He is not to be trusted, I fear; none of them ever were except the old man. I must see what the victim is like; probably she is an ordinary woman, to whom a good name and a higher social position than her own may be all-sufficing."

The next day was ordinary Chicago weather, dull and heavy; but Neale found Wilfred Nevin in high spirits and faultless dress, with dainty gloves and a delicate sprig of gardenia and maiden-hair fern in his button-hole — quite a bridegroom-elect, as Neale told him.

After a second glass of sherry Nevin declared himself ready, and they set out on their important quest.

Arriving at Jackson Park, they at once proceeded to the French art gallery, which was crowded to the doors. Elbowing their way in, Neale looked eagerly round, seeking some figure that might answer to the idea he had formed of Wilfred's intended bride.

There were a variety of visitors : here and there the gay Parisians fluttered in and out among the crowd, pointing out the beauties of "Artemio" by Mons. Wencker, or that ghoulish fable, "Death and the Woodchopper"; here could be seen the stolid German from Unter den Linden, taking side glances at "Saintpierre's Venus" having her sandals put on, the indifferent and lanky Australian with his "bride

from the bush," the weary Cockney gazing
through his eyeglass at "Panaderos," and a
motley but nevertheless interesting crowd of
Austrians, Swiss, Russians, Poles, and in fact
representatives of every nation and clime under the sun. Harold Neale's eyes rolled over
the crowd evidently unsatisfied till they were
arrested by a group which stood before one of
the gems of the collection — a large, breezy
upland covered with trees and grass, some cat-
tle grazing in the foreground and gathering
rainclouds behind. A white-haired, neat old
gentleman was speaking to an elderly woman
who looked as if she might have been housekeeper in a country family. A step or two in
advance stood a slight young girl, whose gown
of fawn-colored alpaca was somewhat short and
scant ; she wore a cape of black cashmere and
a rather broad-rimmed straw hat adorned with
a large bunch of very stiff forget-me-nots ; the
whole costume bore the stamp of Western mil-
linery. A quaint little figure, yet Neale's attention was riveted to it. While he looked Nevin
touched him on the shoulder and exclaimed in a
deep whisper :

"Good heavens ! there she is ! "

Neale smiled at the dismayed expression of his
face.

"How do you know ? " he said.

"Because that is old Watts, the guardian, with her; don't you see him looking round for the other victim?"

"He sees you," said Harold.

Nevin, raising his hat, started forward with a frank, pleasant smile to meet the old gentleman who was beckoning him.

"You are a little behind time, are you not, sir?" said Mr. Watts, in a low tone; "at least it seems a long time since we came into this bewildering place."

"I flattered myself I was rather punctual," said Nevin. "Will you allow me to introduce an old friend of mine, Mr. Neale? I thought it might be as well to make some of my people known to you."

"Certainly, certainly," bowing with ancient politeness; "very happy to know any friend of yours, I am sure. Now—now I will present you. It is really a curious and somewhat daring experiment, but with a man of honor—a —I have no doubt all will go well. My young ward is quite taken up with that picture of Bonheur's. A—A—Alice, my dear," touching her arm. She turned quickly and looked full at him with a startled expression, as if suddenly recalled from another world, showing under her large hat a simple, pale, gentle face, the nose a little upturned, the mouth scarcely

small enough for beauty, the eyes dark, but of
no particular color, the hair light brown and
smooth—an ordinary face enough, but pleasant
and not without a certain attraction.

"Alice, this is Mr. Nevin, the gentleman
who stopped our runaways on Michigan Avenue. Mr. Nevin, Miss Ashland."

She gazed from one to the other and then
took Nevin's hand, saying gently: "You do
not know how thankful I am to you for saving
my life." Nevin bowed, and then, with what
Harold perceived to be an effort, asked : "Is
this your first visit to the Fair ? "

" No, not to the Fair, but this is my first
visit to the art gallery. I never saw many
pictures before, except two or three at home."

" There are quite too many here for comfort ; you will be very tired before you leave."

" I feel a little giddy when I look round,
certainly, but I should like to stay on and on
till I saw every one."

" You must come constantly, taking a rest
between your visits," said Neale, who was determined to make acquaintance with the poor
little heiress.

" I should like to, but it would cost so much.
Mrs. Williams would have to come, too, you
know."

" Still, I think Mr. Watts would not object,"

said Nevin, looking down at her with a caressing smile. "I rather imagine he would find
it difficult to refuse you."

"Mr. Watts—yes, he is very kind, but Mr.
Bond is always unhappy about money," she
returned, quite unconscious of the implied compliment ; and she looked again at the picture.

Nevin seemed checked, and, turning, observed politely to Mr. Watts : "Your friend
looks very tired. I think I can find her a seat."

"I'm sure, sir, you are very polite," said
the weary Mrs. Williams gracefully, and Nevin
escorted her to a seat in the center of the room,
where she sat down with a groan.

"This is a clever picture," said Harold
Neale, who kept his place by Miss Ashland.

"It is wonderful," she said, in a low tone, as
if absorbed in contemplation. Her voice was
soft and her accent fairly good. "I almost feel
the cold breeze that generally comes up with the
rain ; and those distant blue hills, how far away
they look ! That is what I cannot do when I
try to paint ; I cannot make the distance look
far."

"A few months' study with a good master
would help you over that difficulty," said Harold, kindly, a feeling of compassionate interest
drawing him to the speaker. "You are an
artist, then ?"

"I wish I were. Mr. Watts has agreed to let me have lessons, and I shall work hard, so hard."

"Work hard!" echoed Nevin, returning to her side as she spoke. "What a tremendous resolution! May I ask what is the object to be attained?"

Miss Ashland colored slightly and looked down as if she thought he was laughing at her.

"I want to learn drawing," she said, simply.

"Then Mr. Watts must find you a good mas- ter. Has he any idea whom to employ?"

"Oh, I suppose so."

"It's very important to find the right man," said Nevin, gravely. "What master do you think of, Mr. Watts, for Miss Ashland?"

"I really have not an idea on the subject," replied Watts, nervously. "I never had any- thing to do with art or artists. No doubt Mr. Bond, who is almost universally informed, will be able to supply our needs."

"I don't fancy art is much in his line either," said Nevin, with an air of careless superiority. "Now I know one or two good men, and shall be most happy if I can be of use to Miss Ash- land."

"It would be doing me a great service," cried Mr. Watts, with a look of relief. "I have been a good deal troubled how to gratify this whim of my ward's."

"You must not call it a whim," said Nevin, smiling, and looking down at Miss Ashland as if they understood each other. "It is a laudable ambition and a charming taste. Will you allow me to see some of your drawings?"

"Yes; then, if you understand art, you can tell me if I am worth teaching," she returned, with quiet earnestness.

They moved on to look at the other paintings, and Harold Neale noticed that the little California girl was always attracted by the best pictures and showed a wonderful amount of discrimination in her observations.

He remarked that she did not seem to care for human figures and faces.

"I suppose it is because I have seen more of the country and four-footed creatures than I have of people," she returned. "It seems to me that I understand them better. Do you draw?" she asked, with some timidity, looking straight into his eyes as she spoke. "You feel the pictures more than he does," and she looked toward Nevin with a little nod.

"He must know more than I do about art; I do not draw, I only ignorantly worship," returned Harold.

"I am sorry." Something in her voice suggested she would prefer being assisted by him than by his friend.

"You will find no lack of instructors, Miss Ashland."

"The difficulty will be to choose among the multitude," said Nevin.

"Well, my dear," said Mr. Watts, who looked bored to death, and was frequently gazing toward the door, "I suppose you have seen enough for one day, and I—I have an appointment of some importance, a—"

"You are very tired," said his ward, kindly, glancing at him.

"Why lose your time here, then?" asked Nevin, blandly. "We shall be delighted to take charge of Miss Ashland and Mrs. —I did not catch the name—and see them safely en route home."

"If you would be so good," said Mr. Watts, hesitating.

"I do not want to stay much longer," said Miss Ashland, "if I can come soon again. There is a great picture of a chariot race in the next room ; I should like to look at it, then I shall be quite ready to go."

"Then I shall bid you good-afternoon, my dear, and good-by for the present. I am going to Washington for a few days. Meantime, if you need advice or assistance—a—a—you have

my excellent colleague, Mr. Bond, at hand.
Good-day, Mr. Nevin ; good-by, Mr. Neale,"
and with a bow to Mrs. Williams, who was
still nodding in the seat Nevin had found her,
the old gentleman walked away with much
alacrity.

"Poor old fellow ! it is really too bad to drag
him about. Don't you think I might fill the
place of guide, philosopher and friend, and
leave him at peace?" exclaimed Nevin, looking
after him with a smile.

"Thank you, you are very kind. If it would
not be too much trouble I should be so glad to
be shown some of the things I ought to see, and
I don't care about these Fair guides. Mrs. Williams and I feel lost here, and we might almost
as well go about blindfolded as go about alone."

"Good.   Then I shall devote myself to your
service during the remainder of your stay.
What shall we do to-morrow? Can we manage the Chinese Theater, the Japs' Village and
the Australian collection ?"

"If you do, Miss Ashland must have forty
horse-power of sight-seeing and endurance,"
said Neale, laughing.

"I have seen the Australian exhibits and the
Chinese Theater," returned Miss Ashland,
gravely. "I think Mrs. Williams must rest
to-morrow ; but could you take me to a school

of art or a drawing class? We might find
out the cost of lessons and go and tell Mr.
Bond after. Do you know Mr. Bond, too?''

"I have that honor"—with an air of profound respect. Miss Ashland looked quickly
and keenly at him. " The best plan is to per-
mit me to call on you to-morrow, at any hour
you may appoint, and we can arrange our cam-
paign. I shall in the meantime make some inquiries about studios, etc.''

"You are very good, indeed. I feel *so* much
obliged to you.'' The color came slowly, softly
into her cheeks and a very sweet smile parted
her lips. "I am sure Mr. Watts will be very
pleased.''

" Mr. Watts is very dear to me,'' said Nevin,
greatly.

" Is that so ? ''

"Then you must give me your address,'' and
Nevin took out his note-book.

"Two thousand and forty West Halstead
Street,'' said Mrs. Williams, who had scarcely
spoken before, and who now joined them. Her
accent was peculiarly flat and her voice of the.
sing-song description, though her utterance was
rapid.

"Near Garfield Park !'' said Nevin. "Why
did they banish you to so terrible a locality ? ''

"Dear me ! is it that bad ? '' exclaimed Mrs.

Williams, in much dismay. "They're nice rooms and cost enough, I can tell you — eighteen dollars a week and fifty cents extra every time you want a fire."

"The place is perfectly respectable I have no doubt," said Harold Neale, laughing. "My friend Nevin is very fastidious; anything on the West Side appears a savage wilderness to him."

"Don't believe him; he's half a savage himself, Miss Ashland. He has always lived in the wilds."

Miss Ashland looked from one to the other with a puzzled air; then, as if wishing to atone for what seemed to her the rudeness of Nevin's speech, she said softly, with a kind look into Harold's face: "That is no matter; it has not made you rude or wild."

"You little know him!" said Nevin, in tragic tones.

"You are laughing. Do you always laugh?" she asked, uneasily. "Come, Williams, let us go home. I think I know the car we came on, and you are too tired to walk."

"Walk!" exclaimed Nevin—"don't think of it," as they moved toward the entrance; "I will get a coupe."

"No—no—not a coupe, we came in the Cottage Grove Avenue car. Mr. Bond told us to avoid coupes, they cost so much money."

" Mr. Bond is—let us say, over-cautious."

"He is a careful man, sir, and *my* brother,"
put in Mrs. Williams.

" And most conscientious I am sure," said
Nevin, in a peculiar tone. " Still you must let
me insist on the coupe, and I will settle with
the driver."

"No, certainly not!" cried Miss Ashland,
decidedly. " I shall pay for it myself."

" I dare not contradict you. Then at what
hour may I present myself to-morrow ?" asked
Nevin, with an air of profound deference.

"Oh, to-morrow? Well, any time after
nine ; they will not give us breakfast until
8:30," returned Miss Ashland.

Wilfred Nevin gazed at her with so bewildered an expression that Neale could not
resist laughing. " My friend here is not given
to early rising," he said. " He has a terrible
complaint which checks his natural energy—
want of occupation."

"That is very bad, very wearisome," she
returned, gravely. " Will *you* come to-morrow ?" she continued, looking at Harold without a shade of hesitation or embarrassment.

" I am sorry I cannot have that pleasure ; I
have an engagement."

" What ! at nine in the morning ?" said
Nevin.

" Not quite so early."

" Well, Miss Ashland, if I may come after luncheon, say about 2:30, we will arrange some charming plans."

" Thank you; we shall have quite finished dinner by that time."

" You may be sure I shall be punctual."

Here a hack, which Nevin had hailed, drove up.

" Dear me! I hate those things!" cried Mrs. Williams; "you can never see where you are going. I'm always afraid of a collision."

" They are much better than the cars. All the infectious diseases travel in the cars."

" Think of that now! Isn't it a shame? What'll we do, Alice, my dear?"

" Oh, let us take the hack;" she paused, and after a moment's hesitation held out her hand, first to Nevin and then to Neale, with not undignified simplicity.

As the vehicle drove away Nevin passed his arm through Harold's, and they walked down Midway Plaisance in silence for a few paces; then Nevin exclaimed with a groan: "She is even worse than I expected. What a price I shall have to pay for independence! What a figure! What a toilet! Could anything ever lick her into shape?"

" I don't agree with you," returned Harold;

"she is quaint, but far from commonplace. I believe if she were dressed up, like Mrs. Wainwright or your sister, she might even look pretty."

"Like Mrs. Wainwright! Great heavens! what are you thinking of? Did you see her white stockings and charity-school shoes?"

"I did, and I also observed that the ankles so travestied were remarkably neat."

"Why, Harold, you are not going in for rivalship?"

"You are quite safe so far as I am concerned," returned Neale, dryly. "But I doubt if your game will be as easy as you anticipate."

"Easy! it is sure to be hard work in any case; and then this craze for art! I must get Mary to help me there. In fact, I shall never get through the affair without Mary's help; but I can count on her; she wants to get me off her hands."

"Why Wilfred, with your interest and sharpness you ought to be able to make your own living without having to sell yourself."

"Make my own living! what a disgusting phrase! Really, Harold, there is a stronger backwoods flavor about you than I thought. However, I have not committed myself to anything. Old Bond, the snuffy one, wants to make some final conditions before I open the siege in form. By the way, are you to dine with the Cravens on Thursday?"

"I am."

"Then pray tell Mary the enormous sacrifice I am making to a stern sense of duty."

"What duty?"

"The duty of self-maintenance."

"I shall tell her my opinion if she asks it. Now I must leave you."

"Would you come down to Evanston? Mary will be there, and she told me to bring you."

"Sorry I can't, but I have an appointment with a man who wants to rent one of our farms; I am almost late already."

"Well, good-by for the present. If you had any compassion you would not leave me to my sorrow."

"I feel sure you will not long need consolation," said Harold, smiling, as he nodded good-by to his friend at the end of the Plaisance and jumped into a coupe. "It is no affair of mine," he mused, as the vehicle whirled along toward the city, "but I can't help feeling sorry for the girl. But women are strange animals; I cannot take credit to myself for understanding them, though that fellow's sister gave me a lesson or two."

CHAPTER III.

MRS. CRAVEN came down dressed for dinner and entered her beautiful drawing-rooms, her white neck and arms gleaming through the filmy black lace which affected to cover them.

She was ready in good time this especial Thursday, as she hoped for an opportunity of speaking to her brother before Major Craven appeared.

"Wilfred is always late. I do hope he had my note," she thought, as she sank on to a comfortable lounge. Then rousing herself, she leaned forward to glance at the clock, and as she did so Wilfred Nevin was announced. "I was afraid you would not come in time," she exclaimed.

"What is it, Mary? Are you in a scrape?"

"A scrape! *Me?*" she returned, with a large note of interrogation. "That is not likely to happen. No; I want to warn you against confiding this matrimonial venture of yours to Harold Neale. I am half afraid you have done so already."

"Yes, of course I have. Did I not tell you I took him with me to witness my interview with my fiancée, as I consider her?"

"Then you are a greater fool than I took you for. Unless he has changed, Harold is the sort of man who strains at gnats and does *not* swallow camels; that is what that Scotchman, Charley Richards, said about him, and you remember how the deacon used to call him Harold Hardcase. He is quite capable of making love to her himself."

"And cutting me out himself, eh?" added Nevin, laughing at his sister's intimation. "I think you do him injustice; he's not quite such an idiot, though he did vow eternal love to that one-eyed Miller girl at Clallam. You don't suppose he is still the credulous blockhead you bamboozled? I can tell you he is both tough and hard."

"Very likely," returned Mrs. Craven, a faint, almost tender, smile passing over her lips. "Still, he would despise your method of finding a well-dowered wife. I hope you did not let him think *I* knew anything about it."

"Of course I did. Why, I backed myself up with your approbation."

"Really, Wilfred, you are too unprincipled. You cannot really believe that other people have scruples. I am infinitely annoyed. What will Harold Neale think of me?"

"He won't think about you at all; he'll think more about the crease in his new Sunday

pants; and what the deuce would it matter if
he did? He is not horrified—not a bit of it.
He is rather amused at the whole affair. If
anything he is rather taken with my little
Quakeress; says she reminds him of 'Toby
Gooch.' It is only natural, you know, that having been jilted by a lioness, Harold should console himself with a mouse."

Mrs. Craven did not reply at once, but a
flash of vivid anger gleamed in her eyes, a look
that Wilfred knew and never trifled with.

"It would serve you right if he won the
prize from you," she said, quietly. "It is well
you told me. I shall know what line to take.
If," she continued, after another slight pause,
"if I am to assist you, you must consult and
be guided by me. Wilfred, I have not seen you
for nearly a week; have you been absorbed
by your devotion to Miss Ashland, or to—"

"Not altogether," he interrupted, quickly.
"I have escorted her to the Exposition three or
four times and to Lincoln Park and the races,
but my evenings have been my own. She is
raving to go to the theater, but I can *not* stand
that. It is more than any one can stand to
appear in public with the wall-eyed old ghoul
who chaperons her. Your maid, Christina
Croten, would disdain to associate with Mrs.
Williams. You must really help me, Mary,

and educate your future sister-in-law to something near up-to-date before I marry her; and
for Heaven's sake find her a drawing-master, or
a studio. She is a pertinacious little ' cuss,'
and more difficult to make an impression on
than I expected; I wish George O'Brien had
written up the accident instead of that booby
Pringle, whom nature better fitted for some
' Variety Dive,' or freak museum, than the
press.''

" Ah, indeed,'' returned Mrs. Craven thoughtfully. " Well, Wilfred, whenever you've finally
settled with the acting guardian, I will call on
this girl and see what is to be done. I might
ask her here, as Mrs. Wainwright has gone to
do penance with her mother-in-law. But she
must be obedient; she must put herself completely in my hands.''

"Ah, Nevin, it is something to see you in
good time,'' said Major Craven, who had entered unperceived, and now approached them.

He was short and broad, with bowed legs and
anything but a soldierly bearing, and derived
his rank from some raw recruits he mustered,
but never led into the field, during the trials of
the early sixties. An exceedingly red, weather-
beaten face, small, sharp eyes contrasted
strongly with his wife's grace and dignity.

" Yes, I am going to be practical and punct-

ual," returned Nevin, gravely. " In short, I
am going to turn over that new leaf I have been
so long fingering."

" High time you should, my boy."

" Why, Wilfred, you have turned over new
leaves enough to make a large volume," said
his sister.

"Judge and Mrs. Rohde," announced the
butler, and Mrs. Craven went forward to receive them. Mrs. Wainwright and Mr. Neale
quickly followed ; then Mr. James Woods, of the
"Customs," a well-known dining-out man, and
the little party was complete.

Mrs. Craven welcomed Harold Neale with
frank cordiality, and introduced him as an old
playfellow to her husband, who shook hands
with him and said he was very glad to make his
acquaintance. Then, dinner was announced.
Neale took in Mrs. Wainwright, and found her
an amusing companion ; indeed, every one of
the party seemed gifted with the power of saying trifles agreeably in a way that sounded
witty. The time flew in exchange of scandal,
anecdote and political chit-chat, and when the
men rose from the table Major Craven excused
himself from joining the ladies on the plea that
he had to have his smoke. Judge Rohde, the
best-hearted and most genial member of the

bar in the States, but an inveterate smoker, accompanied him.

"Do help me to get Mr. Woods to sing," said Mrs. Craven to her brother, as he came up to her. "Have you ever heard Mr. Woods sing, Mr. Neale? He is a real Nicolini. Nature and art combined. Just one song, please."

"I shall be most happy," and the gentleman, who never lost an opportunity of using his catarrhal tenor, went readily to the piano and warbled out one of Tosti's "Oh sadly sweet and beautifully blue" arrangement of notes, over which modern drawing-room sparrows continue to croak. Mrs. Craven sat profoundly still in her corner of the sofa, her head slightly turned from Harold, showing the graceful outline of her throat and the delicate beauty of her small ear. When the singer ended, with a long-drawn *mee-ow*, Mrs. Craven heaved a deep sigh, and looking round to Neale, who stood near her, smiled as she raised her eyes to his.

"What wonderful pathos he puts into it! It is a voice that pierces the heart, or whatever does duty for that sentimental organ."

"A fine voice," he returned, "but a most doleful ditty. Do you not sing? I think I remember your singing 'Changeless' in what I then considered a heavenly style."

"I never sing now except when I am alone,"

said Mrs. Craven. "When I want to live the past over again I sit down and croon to myself."

She drew her dress closer to her to make room, and with a gesture invited him to sit beside her. Neale obeyed; the rest clustered round the piano discussing De Wolf Hopper's "Panjandrum," morsels of which Mrs. Wainwright played from time to time.

"My dear," exclaimed Major Craven, who, with Judge Rohde, had entered the room unseen; "my dear, the judge and I are going to town for a couple of hours."

"And who is to see me home?" asked the judge's wife.

"Oh, Mr. Woods there will perform that service for me," replied the genial judge.

And bidding good-night to all, the colonel and judge took their departure.

"Tell me," said Mrs. Craven, slowly opening and shutting a large black leather fan, "how is it that my brother has persuaded you to assist him in his extraordinary matrimonial scheme? I did not think you could so completely cast aside the romantic chivalry that used to distinguish you in the days when we were Mary and Harold to each other."

"Romantic chivalry!" repeated Harold, smiling. "1 am not aware I ever possessed such a characteristic. It must have evaporated long ago. But, Mrs. Craven, I had no idea what Wilfred was about until he came and asked me to be present at his second meeting with the young lady whom he intends to appropriate. I confess I was amazed and expressed my astonishment freely ; but you don't suppose any preaching of mine would influence your brother ? "

" No, I do not think any one influences him. But he has been talking to me very seriously about this strange idea of his and has rather won me over. We have had a great deal of anxiety over Wilfred. He is provoking, but lovable. You see, he is one of those unlucky men who can *not* work."

" Indeed ! " said Harold, dryly.

" Ah ! to a man of your energy that must seem impossible or contemptible, but you are quite different. You are—" She stopped, looked down and a soft flush stole over her cheek and throat. " At all events," raising her eyes to Neale's, which were bent on her with calm observation that stung her with an irritating sense that he was the stronger of the two, " at all events, poor Wilfred has cost us a good deal in every way, and really, *if* this girl is not *too* dreadful, it would be well to secure her fortune for my brother. He would

never be a steady husband, nor would he be an
unkind one.   Her money might be tied up, and
they would get on as well as half—two-thirds
of the married people one meets."

"Perhaps," said Harold, half unconsciously,
as the recollection of the innocent, fearless eyes
that looked out from under Miss Ashland's
backwoods hat came back to him with a great
wave of compassion.

"Tell me, what is she really like?" pursued
Mrs. Craven.   "I can depend on what you say
more than on Wilfred's report."

"I do not think my judgment can be of much
use to you, Mrs. Craven ; our ideas must be as
widely different as our experiences.   Miss Ashland is exceedingly rustic, and, even to my un-
instructed eyes, badly dressed, but she is rather
quaint than unladylike ; there is no tinge of
Poverty Flat about her.   She is rather pretty,
so it seems to me."

"Then you think I might make something of
her?"

"Oh, you could do wonders, I have no doubt."

"Ah, Mr. Neale, your tone is cynical, but I
am ready to bear a good deal from you."

This with a smile and upward glance from her
soft-brown, beseeching eyes.

Harold laughed good-humoredly.

"You wrong me.   In sober earnest I believe

you could influence any young girl, if you chose to be kind to her," he said.

"You have grown very hard in these long years of wandering, Harold — forgive me, I mean Mr. Neale."

"My surroundings have certainly not been calculated to soften me " he returned, "but I don't suppose I am harder or stronger than my neighbors. However, I trust if you take up this scheme of your brother's, you will give some consideration to the young lady's interests. I suppose your womanly sympathy will be her safeguard."

"You seem to have espoused her cause very warmly," said Mrs. Craven, looking down.

"I do not think I have, only I like fair play. Remember, it is a game at blindman's buff, with odds of 10 to 1 against the blind man, or rather woman."

"You are right," said Mrs. Craven, gently. "I will promise to be *her* friend as well as Wilfred's."

"I have no doubt you will be," began Harold, when he was interrupted by a demand from vivacious Mr. Woods.

"Do ask Mrs. Wainwright to sing, Mrs. Craven. I am sure she sings, and she is going to steal away to President Potter's ball."

"But I don't sing; I don't do anything but

cumber the earth," said Mrs. Wainwright. "I
always find people to do everything for me
much better than I could do them myself."

"You must pay your shot, however, in one
way or another," cried the lively James.

"Not that I am aware of," replied Mrs.
Wainwright. "I can't pay anything; I am
too disgustingly poor."

"Yet you contribute your share, and a large
one," cried Nevin. "You add the harmoniz-
ing tone, the complimentary touch of color
needed by society." His tone, though light,
had a tinge of earnestness in it.

"My dear Mr. Nevin, you must have been
reading some of Ward McAllister's inane scrib-
blings in the New York *World*. If I get on at
all it is because I am a neutral tint," said Mrs.
Wainwright, coming over to say good-night to
Mrs. Craven. "So sorry not to be with you,
dear. This is a delightful house you've taken
for the Fair season, but I must do the devoted
to the Potters or the result will be insolv-
ency."

Mrs. Judge Rohde and Mrs. Woods were also
taking their departure, and Nevin escorted Mrs.
Wainwright.

"If you can stay a little longer I'll sing you
some of our old favorites," said Mrs. Craven,

as Harold turned to bid her good-evening. "Do
you care to stay?"

So Harold stayed.

Mr. Bond occupied a suite of rooms on the top
story of that world-famed "sky-scraper" known
as the Masonic Temple. The rooms were in
every sense worthy of the occupant, a keen,
shrewd, nervous, yet matter-of-fact Chicago
lawyer, with No. 1 constantly before his mind's
eye. Mr. Bond, with all his keenness, shrewd-
ness and nervousness, had only eked out a
modest living until the news reached him of his
old friend James Ashland's death in far-away
California, and his appointment as executor
and guardian, with Mr. Watts as his second,
to Ashland's only child, a daughter. Two
years after the father's death the girl's uncle
died intestate, and Mr. Bond had the management of the large estate he left. On this occa-
sion of our introduction to Mr. Bond, that
worthy was standing beside his desk holding a
letter, at which he did not look—a small, lean,
angular man, with a large head, sharp little
eyes fenced with spectacles, a wide, thin-lipped
mouth, that seemed forever smiling, and a
short, upturned nose. His lips moved as if repeating something to himself. Presently he
muttered: "Ten thousand dollars; can't vent-

ure to put it higher, anyhow; and that's a poor price." Then he looked at the letter and read it through with a sardonic grin. "Blessed old fossil, it shall have its resurrected mammoths from Dakota, as long as it does not hinder me from gathering shekels. I can manage business affairs better than old Watts, eh? I believe you! Well, it's an ill wind that blows nobody good; even a Chicago wind can't do that. Lord, what fools they all are! Here's another," taking up a second letter and reading: "'When is my darling to come back to me? She'll never be happy among the grand folks at the World's Fair.' (If Kate had an ounce of sense, what a help she might be to me. It's a mercy I have the bit of writing that might ruin her boy. The idiot! I have him and her in my grip pretty fast.) 'Your loving sister, K. Williams.' Bosh! Why the, devil *will* she write? Letters are always dangerous," tearing it into a dozen pieces. "I'll turn her to account, for all her devotion to the girl."

Here a shock-headed office-boy, coming in, interrupted him. "Gentleman, sir," he said, thrusting a card into his master's hand.

"Ha! show him in, and, mind you, I'm particularly engaged. Don't let mortal in, not even Mr. Clay."

The boy nodded and went out, whereupon

Wilfred Nevin entered, perfectly dressed, fresh, cool, good-humored, an extraordinary contrast to Mr. Bond and his surroundings.

"Good-morning, sir, good-morning," said the latter. "Sit down. Warm morning, isn't it? Sun in your eyes?" as he pulled down the blind.

"Pray don't trouble yourself, I'm all right," said Nevin, seating himself.

"Well, well, my dear sir, how are we gétting on?" asked Bond.

"That is what you call a leading question," returned Wilfred, smiling. "On the whole, not badly. I have been doing my duty. I have presented flowers, and they have been joyously accepted. In a couple of weeks or so I may, with your sanction, venture to propose."

"There are just a few preliminaries to settle first," said Mr. Bond, gently scratching his head with the top of his pen. "I asked you to come and talk them over, because Mr. Watts leaves everything to me."

"Oh, I'm perfectly content. You have a masterly way of managing business that is quite remarkable. Pray what are these preliminaries? I thought you had sufficiently inquired as to my walk in life, and found the particulars highly creditable. I had even got rid of my debts before I had the pleasure of meeting your ward, though I warn you they are beginning to accumulate again." .

"That I dare say," returned Bond, with a grin. "I am prepared to stand your friend, and, remember, without my full consent"— here his eyes twinkled gleefully—"*no* man has a chance for three or four years to come. Now I am not going to give it lightly ; and first, are you disposed to make *any* sacrifice to prove you are in earnest ? "

"My dear sir, I really have nothing to sacrifice but my liberty, and liberty paralyzed by want of the almighty dollar is not much to resign."

"Ahem ! true for you," said Bond, with a sigh. "I'm sure it would take a week to tell all the trouble and toil I've had with the Ashland estate, to say nothing of the valuable time it has taken up, and no reward for me. You know old Watts and myself are executors as well as guardians, and every blessed bit of work has fallen to my share. Of course I'd gladly do my best for the minor. My sister and I look upon her as our own child."

Nevin bowed assent.

"As I said," resumed Bond, "I'd do anything for the dear child. But I am a poor man; my time is my money, and I have spent months of it upon her."

"I begin to understand," said Wilfred. "Pray go on."

"You are not a business man, Mr. Nevin," continued the lawyer, with a grin. "You are above these sort of things. But I had a very sensible letter from a young man I once pulled through an awkward fix and who has since shot ahead and made a lot of money. This letter contains an offer of eight thousand dollars if I can find him a suitable wife. But read it for yourself."

Nevin took and read the letter.

"Ah! now I understand you. You wish some remuneration for your valuable time and fatherly care? I really don't see what claim you have on me. If my future wife wishes to bestow any trifling gift in the shape of friendship's offering as a token of gratitude for your disinterested care, I have no objection."

Mr. Bond grinned more amicably than ever.

"And suppose I withdraw my sanction, my assistance, where are *you* ? "

"And suppose I persuade the young lady to dispense with your consent ? " asked Wilfred, with an ineffable air. "What shall you do ? "

"Let her money accumulate until I grant it, and tie it up so tight that you can't touch a cent, without her consent, during her life or after her death."

"But you would not sell her to this—this fellow?" asked Nevin, striking the letter with his finger.

"Why not? He is a good enough fellow, with red hair, not unlike yourself."

"I fancy Miss Ashland would see a difference," he said.

"Maybe—maybe, but that isn't the question. Are you willing to make me an offer? I am foolish enough when I like a man, and I like you, especially when I think you'll make our ward happy, only I musn't—I mustn't allow myself to be weak, for my poor sister's sake as well as my own. Who'll look after me when I'm past my work?"

"I cannot tell, I'm sure. But how do you think it would sound if I were to make your proposition public?"

"I don't know, and don't care much; I am not going to commit myself to writing, and my word is as good as yours, who believed Judge Woodman when he charged Mike McDonald with attempted bribery, and what came of it?"

Nevin laughed. "Really, your candor is quite refreshing. Where do you think I'd find eight thousand dollars?"

"Oh, you'll find that much fast enough, but I want two thousand more. Now, to show you that I'm your friend, I'll agree to aid you for ten thousand dollars, providing you leave the management of the property in my hands when it comes into yours."

"You are an admirable diplomat after the knock-me-down Bismarckian school, Mr. Bond," said Nevin. "I cannot admire your cynical frankness sufficiently."

"It's all very fine talking," returned Bond. "But I have what you want, and as Joe Kuhn says, and he's got rich at the same game, 'If you are in earnest you *must* come to my terms.'"

"Why, I have been here nearly an hour," cried Nevin, looking at his watch, "and it is such a fine day. My time is nearly up. Let us come to some conclusion."

"By all means. It rests with you. You know my terms, and I'm really sorry I can't move an inch from them—not with justice to myself."

"A sense of justice which I imagine never fails you."

"I hope it never will."

"Well, look here, then. I don't mind about the money, but I should like to have the managing of my own affairs. In short—excuse the brutality—but as your friend Joe Kuhn would say, 'I'd rather not have *you* for the middleman.' And Joe got rich, you say, and

52

perhaps some of his clients' orphans went to the poorhouse."

"Don't mention it," said Mr. Bond, with a grin, "though you will regret the prejudice by and by. If I fall in with your views I must have an equivalent."

"What will you consider an equivalent?" cried Wilfred, again looking impatiently at his watch.

"Hum! it is rather hard to say off-hand; but then I will not bargain with a man like yourself — hand me over twenty thousand dol·lars within a week of your marriage and I shall be satisfied."

"Twenty thousand! that's a tremendous haul, and, as you tell me, there is not much ready money. Will not this cramp me?"

"Not a bit of it. That last purchase of old Ashland's, which swallowed up so much ready cash, is worth nearly double what he gave for it. I can get double to-morrow. Then we have the Riverside orange groves, which bring in ten thousand a year. Oh, there's plenty of property; you just sign a little bond, acknowledging yourself my debtor for twenty thousand dollars at five per cent., and matters will go smooth and easy."

"For you, perhaps. But I'm not such an incapable as to put myself completely in your power. Would you trust me, as you ask me to trust you?"

"Ay, don't you be too mistrustful; it is a bad sign, my young friend."

"I will sign no such bond, Mr. Bond, I assure you, unless I can be secured in some way. Why, you might demand payment whether I married or not."

"Why, what have I done that you think me a common cheat?"

"Rather an *un*common one," returned Nevin, contemptuously. "Of course, I mean in an intellectual sense. Show me how I can be secured and I'll sign what you like as to the dollars."

"Dear, dear! what a money-lender was spoiled when you were born a gentleman; how Frank Clapp would admire you!" exclaimed Bond, with an admiring leer.

"Born a borrower instead of a lender, you mean."

"Let me see, how can I satisfy you? I'm that obliging I'd like to make things easy. Suppose when you execute the bond I give you a letter, stating that unless the marriage between you and Miss Ashland takes place the bond is void and you absolved from all obligation of payment."

"Yes, I think that might do; but I should like counsel's opinion on it."

"Ah, what nonsense ! There is no use throwing away a fee. I saw you with Judge Rohde the other day ; ask him ; he is one of the few straight legal lights of modern Babylon ; he'll tell you you are as safe as the Constitution."

"I will," returned Nevin ; "meantime, unless advised to the contrary, it is a bargain."

"Good, good ; I am glad you see your own interest."

"Then I can press on with my suit. By the way, my sister will call on Miss Ashland ; I should like to invite my future wife to stay with her; she will want a good deal of brushing up. If she does, Mr. Bond, I warn you she will ask you for big checks."

"O Lord !" exclaimed Bond, shrugging up his shoulders as if in pain. " Does it cost such a heap to start a young lady ? "

"I fancy the general run of milliners' bills would make you weep. But I have an engagement, so *au revoir*. I suppose I may make all the running I can ? "

"Certainly ; I am as anxious to have her off as you are to get her. You are just the man I sighed for."

"Much obliged to you," said Nevin. "Let

me have a line when the bond and the letter are ready. Good-morning."

"Infernal old fiend," muttered Wilfred, as he went down the elevator.

"Got him sure," chuckled old Bond, as he closed the door.

CHAPTER IV.

"I am getting rather tired of this great shop," said Harold Neale to himself, as he walked with a listless and half-weary step between the rows of showcases in the Swiss Court at the World's Fair one bright afternoon when all the world seemed crowded into this most magnificent of all expositions. The showcases were resplendent with articles of Swiss ingenuity and inventions, which the envious crowd were admiring. "There's not a sight of its kind on the face of the earth," mused Harold, "but I would rather not see it every day unless I had a lot of work to do in connection with it. I would rather be home on the Hudson. There's not much to do even there, but a few days' fishing can always be had. That's something I can enjoy better than this gorgeous crowd."

Suddenly a look of surprised attention replaced the careless glance with which he had eyed the exhibits and crowd, for a few feet from him stood Alice Ashland, gazing admiringly at an exhibit of tiny watches. He was startled to see her alone in that motley crowd. Country bred as he was, it seemed unbecoming for a lady to be alone in such a crowd, and he hastened to give her the protection of his companionship.

"Miss Ashland, may I hope you remember I was introduced to you by—"

"Oh, yes," she interrupted, with a bright, startled look of surprise and pleasure. "I am very glad to see you. I was just beginning to feel lonely, even here, and the place is rather puzzling and you will show me around."

"I shall be most happy to assist you in any way. How is it that you are alone?" asked Harold, gravely.

"Mrs. Williams is not quite well to-day. So I walked down Halsted Street, and suddenly the impulse seized me to come again to the Fair, for I like looking at the exhibits, everything is so very beautiful."

"I shall certainly escort you about the place and see you safely home. It is not quite safe for you to be alone in Chicago."

"Why? There is nothing to fear. I take

very little money, and no one ever interferes with me."

"Still I do not like to see you by yourself. Suppose we have an outing on the lake in one of the Venetian gondolas ? "

"Oh ! I'm so much obliged. That would be splendid, and something entirely new to me."

They left the building and seated themselves in one of the gondolas, which its picturesque gondolier shot hither and thither through the numerous canals, to the infinite delight of Miss Ashland, who declared on their way home that she had never spent such a delightful afternoon since she left California. Leaving the Fair grounds Harold hailed a coupe, and they started homeward.

"I suppose you ride when you are at home ?" began Harold, who was curious to learn something of her past.

"Not now. When I had my father with me we had a nice pony, and I used often to ride on him. But one day afterward, you know " (he understood that she meant after her father's death), "Mr. Bond came to Santa Cruz and saw poor old ' Billy ' feeding behind the house. Then he said he was no use, and sold him, and let the place to strangers, so we have only the garden and orchard now."

"I daresay you were sorry for the pony."

"Sorry? I *was* sorry! It made me hate Mr. Bond," emphatically. "Indeed, I shall never like him, I have told him so; but I am almost inclined to forgive him for sending my good, kind Williams to live with me. I do not know what would become of me without her."

"It is rather alarming to hear a young lady confess that she hates any one."

"Is it? Well, I did hate Mr. Bond, and I hated the doctor at Santa Cruz. I cannot nor could not help it. I believe I had a bad temper."

"Has time changed it, or have you nobly struggled to overcome your own evil nature?" asked Neale, looking down with a smile at the sweet, thoughtful face beside him.

Miss Ashland laughed a low, pleasant laugh. "I'm afraid not; I grew stronger, and did not need the doctor, and as I felt better and brighter and able to enjoy myself I forgot Mr. Bond. Now he is going to let me learn drawing, and I feel almost friendly toward him."

There was a pause. Harold thought, with growing interest and sincere compassion, that this was not a nature to be satisfied with the shams of society and the paste diamonds of a showy setting to life. Still Nevin could be very fascinating, and she might believe him the best of men, nor have her faith disturbed all the days of her life.

"If Mrs. Williams is well enough to see me, perhaps you will let me look at some of your drawings when we reach your rooms?"

"Yes, I will, gladly. I can draw very little now, but I am to go to a studio on Michigan Avenue, at least I hope so. They have promised to get Mr. Bond's consent."

"Who have promised?"

"Mr. Nevin and his sister. Do you know that he brought his sister to see me? Was it not good of him? And she—" a look of infinite pleasure and admiration beaming over her face—"oh, she is lovely! she is like a queen, and so kind to me, a mere ignorant Western girl. She has asked me to stay with her while I am studying, and says she will do all that is necessary for me. Is it not wonderful?"

"Ah!" ejaculated Harold, "you mean Mrs. Craven. She is certainly charming. When do you go to stay with her?"

"I'm not quite sure. I should have gone on Monday, but Mrs. Williams was unwell and I could not leave her; indeed, that is the only drawback. I do not like her being alone—she

will fret —but she says she does not mind. I
think Mr. Bond has told her she must
not."

So Mrs. Craven was not letting the grass
grow under her feet in the prosecution of her
brother's plan. How would it end for the
guileless Californian, who was probably looked
upon by both as a mere incumbrance to her own
wealth? What would be the result of Mrs. Craven's training? what of associations of Wilfred Nevin? How much of her fearless candor,
her outspoken truthfulness, would be left after
three or four years of life under their guidance?
Harold was conscious of almost fatherly compassion and tenderness toward his young companion, and yet he could do nothing to help or
save her; his interference would be worse than
useless. If he could induce Mrs. Craven to es-
pouse her cause? But could he? He thoroughly distrusted that charming personage,
although she still had fascination for him. At
any rate he would call on her and endeavor to
find her real disposition toward the lonely little
heiress.

All this passed through his brain rapidly, and
he said aloud : "Mr. Bond appears a very potent person."

"He is," said Miss Ashland, with a little
sigh. "I cannot get any money except by his

consent. I do not know what he will think of all Mrs. Craven talks of buying for me."

"I have no doubt Mrs. Craven will manage him, if any one can."

More desultory but friendly, sympathetic talk brought them to the door of Miss Ashland's temporary abode.

" Will you come in ? " she said ; and Harold, with an odd feeling that he was in some way trespassing, followed her into a rather nicely furnished room of the " Rooms-to-let " order.

" If you will sit down for a moment I will see how Mrs. Williams is." She pointed to a chair and left the room.

" What an abode for an heiress !" thought Harold, glancing round at the furniture and narrow space. "I don't suppose she has the faintest idea of her own possessions. She ought to be informed. I'm half inclined to tell her myself. I earnestly hope they will tie up her money strictly when she marries Nevin ; for I suppose she must, she can hardly escape." He took up a book, it was Lew Wallace's "Ben Hur"; he took up another, "Little Dorrit." He looked inside the cover and found the name "James Ashland." "A volume from the family library, I suppose," he said to himself, with a smile.

At this point in his meditations Miss Ashland

re-entered. She had removed her hat, and
Harold observed how much better and more
distinguished she looked without it. Her head
was small and well poised, and her hair, though
pale in color, was abundant, while the gentle
composure of her manner and movements gave
her dignity.

"I must not ask you to stay," she said. "I
find Mrs. Williams so unwell I must attend
her; and the dressmaker sent by Mrs. Craven
is waiting for me."

"Then I will not trespass any longer; I hope
to have another opportunity of seeing your
drawings. As you know Mrs. Craven, I may
see you at her residence."

"I hope I shall. You are very good to have
come all this way with me. Good-by; and tell
me, what is your name? I did not heed Mr.
Watts when he introduced you."

"My name is Neale."

"I think I did not notice your name because
I was taken up with the sort of likeness I saw
about your eyes to my father's. Good-by."

She held out her hand with a grave, kindly
smile. Harold took and lightly pressed it.

"If I can ever do anything for you," he exclaimed, with a sudden impulse, "pray remember that I am at your service." Then, half
ashamed of his speech, he beat a rapid retreat.

"Every one is very good to me," was Alice Ashland's reflection, as she hurried away to the grand-looking, overdressed dressmaker, of whom she was a little afraid, and submitted to the ordeal of "trying on," having been previously measured under Mrs. Craven's eye. Faithful, however, to her suffering friend, she begged leave to show herself to Mrs. Williams before she took off the garment.

"Is it not pretty?" she exclaimed, drawing up the blind that Mrs. Williams might see clearly. "The skirt is to be trimmed with a quantity of the same lace, and bows of brown satin ribbon; they look lovely against the tussah silk. This is called a simple morning dress! It seems to me too fine to wear. I wonder what Mr. Bond will say?"

"Ah! he won't mind now," returned Mrs. Williams, with a sigh so deep it was almost a groan, and would certainly have attracted Alice's attention had she not been hurrying back to the dressmaker.

"You seem worse than you were this morning, dear," she said, returning presently in her every-day dress, "and you look as if you had been crying."

"Well, you see, the pain has been very bad and I am that weak—"

Here the poor woman broke down.

"I will get you some beef tea and a glass of wine, and then I will try this wonderful stuff. It is a whitish stick, and it is to be rubbed on your brow until the pain goes." And Alice went swiftly and silently to and fro, procuring the remedies she had suggested, and Mrs. Williams grew more composed.

"Whatever will I do without you, Alice? The sight of you does me good."

"I will not leave you till you are quite well and strong."

"Ay, but you must, my dear. Brother Bob has been here while you were out"—a half-suppressed sob.

"Oh!" cried Alice, "he has been here! Then he has been scolding you. What did he say?"

"Well, he was a bit nervous, but always anxious about *you*, miss, my dear. And do you know he has even been to see that Mrs. Craven about you? And you are to go to her Saturday or Sunday. I am to be sent home because Chicago doesn't suit me, so Bob says. He has grown wonderful careful of my health all at once"—in a querulous tone. "How *he* comes to know such grand people as that Mrs. Craven and her brother is more than I can tell. Says he knew them before the accident; anyhow,

they are very nice and civil spoken, and Mr.
Nevin is very brave, I'm sure."

"Yes, they are very delightful; but I'm not
going to leave you, or to be ordered about by
Mr. Bond," cried Alice, indignantly.

"Ah, but you must, my dear. Bob is in real
earnest about it. He had up the landlady and
gave her warning on the spot, and we are to
be out of this, if I'm all right, by noon on Saturday."

"Well, Williams, I will not stay long; I will
come home soon to you."

"Ah, my dear, it's little I'll see of you from
this time forth forevermore," cried poor Mrs.
Williams, who was apt to grow Scriptural in
her sorrow.

"Why, where am I to be sent?" said Alice,
laughing. "I cannot be kept out of my own
home in Santa Cruz."

"Ah! you'll soon be finding another home
among all these fine people."

"They are too fine for me," said Alice, putting out her writing things. "I feel quite stupid among them. It will be a long time before
I find another home."

And she began to write rapidly.

"You remember the other gentleman that
Mr. Watts introduced to us," she resumed—"I
mean the dark one?"

"Yes, a quiet, grave man."

"I met him to-day and he rode all the way back with me. I like him so much! He is serious and gentle; he does not laugh at everything like Mr. Nevin, and he speaks to me as if I were a reasonable being. I could tell him anything! It is curious, but he gives me the idea that he is sorry for me. He reminds me of my father when he used to look far away and stroke my head, saying: 'Poor child—poor child!'"

"Well, miss, don't you go and trust any one too much, least of all a man. They are a selfish lot the best of them. Now, dear, I'll try and sleep a bit."

Alice Ashland had led a singularly secluded, monotonous life. She had been the sole companion of her widowed father. When he died he left his little all to his daughter—a pretty residence among the redwoods of Santa Cruz and about a thousand dollars a year—appointing his only friends, Mr. Watts and Mr. Bond, her guardians. Bond, having a sister for whom he wished to provide without cost to himself, sent her to his ward in California as the cheapest mode of maintaining both. About two years before the beginning of this narrative her uncle died intestate and she became the owner of considerable wealth, as we have stated. Alice herself knew little or nothing about it. Mr. Watts had told her, but no alteration had been made in her mode of life. To Bond this change in his ward's circumstances was a positive torment. His grasping fingers itched to clutch some of the riches they could touch but not take. To find a suitable (?) husband for his ward before she reached the independence of majority was the object nearest his heart, and we have already seen how accident favored his hitherto baffled search.

It was a trial for Alice to part with Mrs. Williams, who had become greatly attached to her; and it was also something of a trial to go to Mrs. Craven's, but a trial not unmixed with pleasure.

Though all her life a recluse, Alice Ashland was not shy; she was naturally brave, and disposed to trust her fellow-creatures.

"I will write often and tell you everything; you may be sure I will! You know I love writing; and do—do write to me! If you are not well I will come to you, I *will*, whatever Mr. Bond chooses to say."

So with many kisses, Alice bade her good old companion farewell, and took her seat in a respectable-looking carriage, which, to her surprise, had been engaged by Mr. Bond's directions to convey her to Evanston.

Mrs. Craven was at home and alone to receive her. She was ushered into that lady's private sitting-room, a delightful apartment, looking into a beautiful garden, and furnished with all that could charm the eye.

"Ah, Miss Ashland! I am so pleased to see you," cried Mrs. Craven, rising to greet her with great cordiality.

"It is really very good of Mr. Watts to trust you with me! But we shall take care of you!" And she drew forward a low easy-chair. "You are looking pale and tired; I am sure you must be moped to death."

"You are very, very kind to ask me here," said Alice, earnestly. "I am so different from you that I may be tiresome, but—"

"I shall turn you out with inexorable cruelty if you are!" interrupted Mrs. Craven, laughing; "but I do not anticipate such a catastrophe! Now you must leave all worry behind you; and do you know your eyes look suspiciously like tears!"

"Yes, I did cry a little," said Alice, coloring. "I was so sorry to see Mrs. Williams go away alone. I have never been away from her since she came to me, nearly eight years ago."

"Very sweet and nice of you, dear, but it is time you broke away from this incongruous companionship. That good old woman was only fit to be your nurse! You need not discard her, but you have been shamefully neglected and kept in the background. Now you must be introduced into society suited to your fortune and position.

"I am afraid I am not suited to any society, except that of a few people whom I like and understand. It is a great pleasure for me to look at you and listen to you; I wonder if I shall ever be able to paint you!" said Alice, with simple earnestness.

"I wish you a better subject," said Mrs. Craven, laughing, though she felt flattered by this honest and unstinted admiration. "Mme. Abbott," she continued, "has sent some of your things, and I see you have put on one of her dresses. Now, come with me and I will show you your room."

Alice followed her hostess upstairs to a pretty, comfortable room, where were laid out what seemed to Alice an enormous amount of clothes—clothes, too, of a superb description. Delicate silks, gauzy grenadines, fairylike hats, coquettish mantles. "What a quantity of money they must have cost!" she cried, aghast. "What *will* Mr. Bond say?"

"That you have a right to the common necessaries requisite for a young lady who is to live like other people," said Mrs. Craven, care-

lessly ringing the bell as she spoke. Her
summons was almost immediately answered by
a young woman. "There, my dear Miss Ashland, is your especial maid! She will attend to
your toilet. Johnston, you had better do
Miss Ashland's hair before luncheon; she has
been living among the redwoods of California,
and I trust to *you* to do her justice."

At lunch the only guest was Nevin, who did
his best to be fascinating; and then came a
crowning joy. Mrs. Craven ordered her carriage and conveyed Alice to a studio, where she
feasted her eyes with the drawings, water-
colors and beautiful objects scattered about,
while Mrs. Craven arranged terms with Signor
Lucca, a fashionable artist, who for a high remuneration instructed Chicago society ladies to
sketch and paint. They then drove to the Fair
grounds, and thence to the city, did some shop-
ping at the famous Marshall Fields, and Alice,
exhilarated by the unusual movement and variety, found herself quite equal to the ceremony
of dinner, as she had never seen dinner served
before; an introduction to Major Craven, who
was quite ready to accept his wife's new favorite unquestioning, as he never interfered with
her as long as she left him alone and did not
spend too outrageous a quantity of money.

Meanwhile, Harold Neale still loitered by the

magical "White City" on Lake Michigan, unwilling to leave. He was strong and penetrating enough to be not one whit blinded by Mrs. Craven's real nature, and yet her beauty, her grace and her evident desire to atone in some way for her past heartlessness dazzled and fascinated him. Harold had long ago ceased to feel the smallest anger against her, and there was a dash of contempt in the plenary absolution he had extended to his old love, Mary Craven.

"Why should I dislike her for being what she *is* rather than what I thought her?" had been his reflection years back; and however brilliant she might be, the core of his opinion was unaltered. But Mrs. Craven's beauty and softness appealed to his senses, and Harold's were still fresh and keen. He could not help the resisted consciousness that his old love was not indisposed to sob out her penitence in his arms; and he knew—none better—how sweet those ripe red lips of hers used to be in the delightfully delusive old days when they sat by banks of the Hudson.

He therefore found it very pleasant to drop in now and then to dinner, though he scarcely went as often as he was asked.

There was now a fresh motive for his visits to Evanston. He was also anxious to see how

Nevin's suit prospered ; how the little flower bore the atmosphere of the splendid hothouse to which she had been transplanted.

Mrs. Craven was dispensing tea to Mrs. Wainwright, Nevin, Miss Ashland, a youthful New Yorker and a very thick-set, elderly man, with a small allowance of neck, who breathed with a snoring sound and drank his tea noisily. Alice was sitting a little apart, busy with some fancy-work. Harold could hardly believe that dress could have so improved any face and figure without destroying its individuality. A gown of soft, creamy material all ruffled with foamy lace ; her soft hair arranged *a la* Langtry. She looked like a modest primrose, and had in no way lost her air of delicate quaintness.

Harold felt a sense of refreshment as his eyes fell upon her, and she met them with a sudden brightening of her own as she rose to meet him with an honest, unconcealed expression of pleasure.

"Mr. Neale, I thought you had left the Windy City," cried Mrs. Craven, holding out her hand. "What has become of you, and what have we done that you should cut us in this way ? "

"I have been wandering to and fro, as usual, and feeling a good deal out of my element,"

returned Neale, making his way to Miss Ashland after greeting Mrs. Wainwright and
Nevin. "I scarcely knew you as I came in,"
he said; "such a complete transformation is
confusing."

"Yes," said Nevin, "you can see that Mary's
reforming fingers have swept the lines where
rust had lingered."

"Really, Wilfred, you are absolutely bru-
tal!—to associate rust with anything half so
ethereal as Alice is too absurd," exclaimed Mrs.
Craven.

"The necessities of rhythm obliged me to
curtail the word rustic. Miss Ashland is strong
enough to bear the truth from her most devoted ally. May I not say so?"

This in a caressing tone and with a lingering
glance.

"Indeed you may! Any one can see I am a
rustic, and will most probably always be one,"
said Alice, with a good-humored smile. "But
I should be dull indeed if Mrs. Craven could not
improve me."

"And what do you think of the theater?"
asked Harold, who had drawn a chair beside
Alice.

"I like it better than anything except the
Fair and the studio, and even better than

either, sometimes," she said, earnestly. "I cannot sleep afterward, it seems so real to me. I think over it, and feel so glad the people are made happy at last. I have never seen a tragedy; I do not think I could bear one."

"You had better realize the unreality of the drama before you risk it," returned Harold, smiling. "And how is Mrs. Williams? I trust she is better."

"I hope so—I think so; at least she does not complain in her letters; but she must be lonely without me. But I shall go back to California when the studio closes."

"When may that be?"

"At the end of August."

"And how are you getting on?"

"Slowly, very slowly; yet I have some hope I may draw pretty well yet. Will you come to the studio some day with Mr. Nevin? He is so kind; he often comes and escorts me home. Is it not good of him?"

"Very good, indeed," returned Harold, while with eyes cast down he thought: He has made no impression as yet; her unconsciousness proves that. "Then you must be very well employed, with art in the morning and gadding about the Fair or the city the rest of the day," he added, aloud.

"Mrs. Craven would make any one happy,

and I never knew what it was to live before.
I was happy enough, but only half awake."

"Then have you turned your back on the
humdrum routine of country life forever?"

"No; I should not live quite as Mrs. Craven
does. I like to go to bed when she goes out in
the evening; but I love the theaters and picture galleries of the Fair and driving in the parks.
Then every one is very good to me, only I do
not always understand what they are talking
about. I am never quite sure if they are in
earnest. Of course, I am very ignorant. I believe I should be happier in the country. I
mean to have my home there."

"There is little that is homelike in either
New York or Chicago life," said Harold; and,
after a pause, he asked: "Who is the stout
gentleman?"

"He is a friend of Mrs. Wainwright's; she
brought him here a few days ago. He is a Mr.
Smith, I think; but Mrs. Wainwright calls him
by some funny name. He has lived a long
time in Australia, I think, and he is very rich."

"What treason are you and Harold hatch-
ing?" said Nevin, coming over and interrupting them. "My sister suggests we go to town,
taking in the Fair en route, dine at 'Rector's,'
and then take in the Coghlans in 'Diplomacy.' Will you come, Neale?"

"Yes, you must," cried Mrs. Craven. "We
shall want three gentlemen; Major Craven is
otherwise engaged, and I shall be all unguarded
if you will not come and take care of me."

Of course Harold consented.

Nevin escorted Miss Ashland, Mrs. Wainwright, somewhat to Harold's surprise, pairing
off with the "Kangaroo," as she called him,
while he himself fell to Mrs. Craven. How
beautiful she looked! How brightly she talked!
What subtle touches of tenderness sounded
through her lighter tone!—and yet Harold was
unusually indifferent. His imagination would
stray away after Alice Ashland and the man
who had appropriated her. Was he teaching
her to love him, with the finished art of long
experience?—and when he had won her heart,
and annexed her money, how would he repay
her? The sense of profoundest pity, of guilt
even—for did not his knowledge of the whole
scheme make him an accomplice?—oppressed
him, and he was powerless to assist her. She
was so defenseless, so friendless! Why, it
would be better for her to marry him.

Mrs. Craven's voice awoke him from his
reverie. "Your judgment was the right one,"
she was saying, as the curtain fell on the
second act of "Diplomacy." "Your little
protegée is really very nice. Naturally a lady,

but frightfully neglected ; she does not seem to 'catch on' to Wilfred's love-making, and he is really most persevering. I think if she were a little responsive he would grow quite fond of her. Really, men are so accustomed to be made love to now that—" She paused.

"It must be rather an agreeable change to do the love-making one's self," said Harold, laughing.

"To men like you, yes—but joking apart, I am really interested in Miss Ashland ; I want them married before we return East. Really Wilfred is nearly at the utmost ends of his resources."

"And suppose Miss Ashland proves so unenlightened as not to appreciate Wilfred ?"

"Now, Harold "—with a deprecating glance —"do not be a bird of evil. She *must* marry him ! "

"Dearest Mary," said Mrs. Wainwright, in an aside quite inaudible to Neale, "I cannot stand the 'Kangaroo' any longer. Do take him off my hands, and let me have a turn with your brother."

So for the rest of the evening Miss Ashland was in Harold's charge, and both felt better for it.

CHAPTER V.

IT was no longer difficult to attract Harold Neale to the Craven residence. He was ready to come on the slightest provocation. He was due home, yet he lingered.

Never had Mrs. Craven been so generally kind and considerate. Alice thought her an angel disguised in a fashionable exterior. Her brother rejoiced in the spell of sunshine, though he had a shrewd idea why "Mary was so amiable." Harold saw too clearly the utter indifference which underlay Nevin's apparent devotion to Alice; he fancied that some instinctive recognition of this was at the root of Miss Ashland's easy, unmoved friendliness. For Nevin was a favorite with women, and what was there to guard that simple, untaught girl from his influence but instinct?

He felt, without the slightest disrespect to her, that had he a fair field he might have won her heart and made her happier than Wilfred Nevin ever could. Her girlish curiosity and frank questioning about himself, his history, his people, half amused him. Had he both father and mother living?—and sisters?—he was rich indeed !

"Mrs. Craven was like a mother and sister to me ; but," added Alice, looking down, " I feel in an odd way that sometime or other I shall pass out of her life, and she out of mine ; the longer I know her, the more I feel how unlike we are, and when she has time to see it, too, she will not like to be bored."

"At present you are a prime favorite, so let the morrow take care of itself," returned Harold ; "you are too natural and truthful to bore any one."

" Do you think so ? I am very glad "—looking candidly into his face ; and Harold thought how charming it would be to see those eyes avoid his with the dawning consciousness of love—love for him only.

Time, however, waits neither for men nor their wooing, and Nevin thought he had served long enough for Rachel ; so regardless of his sister's warning not to be rash, and without her knowledge, he persuaded Miss Ashland to stay at home one afternoon to see some Hungarian photographs he had purchased for her. This afforded him an excuse for a tete-a-tete ; and then, to Alice's immense surprise, with much fervor he made her an offer of his hand and heart and high social position.

When Mrs. Craven returned sooner than was expected she found the brother pacing to and fro in deepest anger and despair.

"The ignorant little savage!" he exclaimed. "I made a confession of my feelings that would have moved the Sphinx. It would have melted the heart of an Apache, and the little wretch was simply surprised, confused, overwhelmed; yet she told me coolly she thought I had mistaken my own feelings—that she was quite sure I liked Mrs. Wainwright better than I did herself! that she was too—too something or other to be my wife, and that she liked me so much she would rather marry some one else."

"Well, Wilfred, you are a greater fool than I took you for," said his sister, frowning sternly.

Could it be the same face that looked up so tenderly in Harold Neale's?

"You tried to shake the tree before the fruit was ripe; now you have lost the game. What do you intend to do?"

"To do! How do you mean? I acted on your instructions and made an ass of myself to no purpose. By Heaven, I shall lose my character if it is known that I have failed with the unsophisticated one."

"You must *not* fail," Mrs. Craven returned. "I must repair your mistake. I wonder I have the patience to speak to you; you have been a worry to us all your life. *Now* you must be absolutely guided by me."

"If you explain your plans I'll try and take them in," said Nevin, who was considerably crestfallen.

"Very well. Leave Miss Ashland to me for the present. I will describe your heartbroken condition and rouse her compassion. You must go out of sight somewhere; it will be the best and safest way of showing your despair."

"But, Mary, I cannot go without cash and I tell you I haven't a dollar. You must get Craven to ante up."

"It would be no use to ask him and I would not do it if it were," returned his sister. "The major has been very generous, but you have tried his patience too far. I want his help myself; I have gone far beyond my allowance. Mme. Abbott has sent me in a hideous bill."

"Then you must give me some cash yourself. I will run over to New York and Newport, and I must pay hotel bills, etc."

"You shall not go to either place," she interrupted. "You shall go and bury yourself at Peekskill, and I will lend you the fare."

"Great Heavens, Mary! What on earth am I to do at Peekskill? I shall cut my throat."

"Better do that than live on a beggarly gentleman," cried Mrs. Craven. "However,

I don't mean to keep you long in exile; and there is tolerable fishing."

"I hate fishing," ejaculated Nevin.

" Old Mrs. Gibbons the housekeeper is a very fair cook. In a week or two I will bring our little startled fawn to hear reason, then you can come back and do exactly as I bid you."

"Ought we to communicate with that old screw, Bond ? "

" I will see Mr. Bond."

" Well, I suppose you have no more to say?"

" No. I never was so angry with you before. " Really, Alice Ashland is too good for you. I suspect you have been betraying your absurd fancy for Mrs. Wainwright more recklessly than I imagined, to rouse Alice's suspicions."

"Not more recklessly than you have shown your absurd fancy for Harold Neale. If I were Craven—"

" You would be a better man than you are," interrupted Mrs. Craven, quietly ; but her eyes darkened and she grew pale with anger ; "and not put evil constructions on a simple natural liking for an old friend."

Nevin laughed aloud cynically.

" If you defy and irritate me," said his sister, rising and standing erect before him, " I shall give you up ; hitherto I have been weak enough to care what became of you. If I turn against you, it will be an exceedingly bad day for you, Wilfred Nevin." She opened her purse and threw him a couple of bills. "I expect you to repay me, remember. Now go ; I will write to Snooks in time for the mail."

She turned from him with a look of contempt and left the room.

Mrs. Craven paused in her own sitting-room and took up some notes and letters, glancing through them mechanically. "I will not speak to her yet," she thought. "Let her chew the cud of sweet and bitter reflection for a while. What a misfortune to have two such idiots to deal with. How did I come to have such a brother?" What was Alice Ashland doing? Sitting in her room in a bewildered frame of mind. What would Mr. Watts say? Nevin had intimated that he had secured her guardian's consent. Would every one be angry? Then she wondered why she had refused him. It was curious, for he was nice and good-looking. Next, fancy suggested: "If Harold Neale had asked you to be his wife would you have refused ?" Conscience instantly answered : " No." Of course, he'd never think of asking her.

At last her maid rapped at the door to say Mrs. Craven had come in and wished to know if Miss Ashland would not have tea.

"No, thank you; I have a bad headache and will lie down till dinner-time," said Alice.

"Shall I bring you a cup of tea here, miss?"

"If you please," returned Alice, eager to be left alone.

Then Mrs. Craven broke in upon her on her way from her dressing-room to the carriage and a solemn dinner party.

"Oh, yes! certainly better."

"Try to eat some dinner or supper and get to bed early. I hope to find you quite well to-morrow morning. Good-night, dear."

A gentle kiss accompanied by a sigh and Mrs. Craven was gone.

Alice seldom saw her hostess in the morning before she went to the studio. Her uneasiness and fearful looking forward to the meeting that awaited her was prolonged, after a disturbed night, through the hours that preceded lunch. Nevin had disappeared.

At luncheon there was only Mrs. Craven, who received her kindly, but with a subdued and pensive air. "I feel quite good for nothing to-day," she said. "I shall not be at home to any one, and at five we will take a drive through Jackson Park. There are a few people coming to dinner and I must brace myself for my duties."

"It will be very pleasant," said Alice, scarcely daring to look up.

"It is a farce, your sitting down to table," said her hostess. "You are looking pale, too, dear. You must see Dr. Secomb."

"I think I feel nervous," faltered Alice.

"Come with me. We will repose ourselves in my room and have a nice long talk."

Alice followed her as if to execution.

"It is certainly delightful to be quiet sometimes," began Mrs. Craven, sinking into a chair. "I know you have a great deal to tell me, a great deal you ought to tell me," continued Mrs. Craven, slowly fanning herself; "but it is difficult to begin. My brother has told me that you refused him, and I am awfully sorry about it all."

"So am I," said Alice, coloring deeply. "I have been deeply distressed, and so afraid you would be angry with me."

"Angry with you! Why should I be angry? Very disappointed, I own, but not angry. But I am, of course, very, very sorry for poor Wilfred! You seemed to like him, and might unconsciously have misled him."

"But, dear Mrs. Craven, I did—I do like him, only I never dreamed he would have thought of marrying *me!* I am sure *you* do not."

"I did not *think* it, because I learned some weeks back that he wished to marry you."

"And you were not vexed, you did not think him foolish?" cried Alice, in astonishment.

"No, dear! Listen to me, Alice. I am worldly. I have hard edges here and there, but I am really very fond of you. Now there is much in you that would be of infinite use to my brother. He took to you at *once*, and that is an unusual thing for him. I am therefore wofully disappointed when my pretty air-castle crumbled at the touch of your cruel fingers."

"You are too good, too indulgent to me," said Alice. "But I do not think I could ever love Mr. Nevin, and I fancied he was very fond of Mrs. Wainwright, which seemed much more natural."

"Of Mrs. Wainwright?" echoed Mrs. Craven. "How very absurd! They are very old friends, and in a sense he is very fond of her; but love, my dear, that's another matter."

There was a pause.

"My greatest regret," began Alice again, "is to have disappointed you in any way."

"I'm glad to hear you care a little for me, Alice. I think I deserve it from you. But not so much as Wilfred. Could you have seen him yesterday I think you would have been sorry for him.' He was so broken-hearted! 'Whatever happens, Mary,' he said, 'do not worry Alice, do not in any way resent my disappointment.' He talks of going to China or Calcutta, or some other dreadful place; indeed, I did not believe Wilfred could have felt anything so intensely; he was as white as a sheet." Mrs. Craven fanned herself vigorously, as if much moved.

Alice trembled, and the tears rose to her eyes.

"I wish I had never come to be a trouble to you!" she sobbed. "What a return this is for all your goodness, and Mr. Nevin's bravery in saving my life! I am very grateful to him for caring so much for me, but—"

"Oh! I suppose he could not help *that*," interrupted Mrs. Craven, with a sad smile. "I know that some time ago he explained his intentions fully to your guardians, and secured their full consent, so that no difficulty should occur in case he could win yours."

"What shall I do? what shall I do?" said Alice, unconsciously aloud.

"Are you in earnest when you ask what you shall do, Alice?" asked Mrs. Craven; "and will you believe that I am disinterested in the advice I offer?"

"Believe *you!* Of course I believe you thoroughly."

"Then let matters stand as they are. Poor Wilfred has run away to bury himself in solitude. I begged him to go to our farm on the Hudson and recuperate. There, I will not say any more at present; but for your own sake, do not throw my brother away too readily, or without some consideration. Of course it is very likely he may not come near us again while you are here. But should he do so—"

She paused, and poor Alice, who felt as if some invisible net was closing round her, urged timidly :

"I suppose one ought to love the man you marry very much ?"

"You should certainly not *dis*like him! But why do you not like Wilfred? Do you love any one else?" with a sudden, almost fiercely questioning glance.

"How could I? Whom do I know to love?" asked Alice, timidly.

"Very true. There, I really think we have exhausted the subject, and you have made your eyes red. Go and bathe them, dear, and do not be unhappy ; I shall always be your friend."

"Ah! do, do be my friend; I have so few," and Alice ventured to pass her arm through Mrs. Craven's and to press her brow against her shoulder with more of a caress than she had ever dared before.

"Oh ! rest tranquil, my dear girl. I am very loyal."

Alice hurried away, and Mrs. Craven, rising to fetch Zola's latest from the table, looked after her with a slight sigh.

CHAPTER VI.

"I must dine at the Cravens to-night," thought Harold Neale, as he stood on the deck of one of the steamers that ply between the World's Fair and the city; "but I will get away home on Monday. I am making a fool of myself here."

On reaching the Grand Pacific, however, where he was stopping, he found a letter which compelled an earlier start. It was from his father, informing him that his mother had taken a chill and had been attacked with the dreaded pneumonia, and it would be well if he could return home at once. Harold was startled; something in the tone of the communication alarmed him.

Mrs. Neale was a gentle, fragile woman. When Harold was in disgrace with all the world she had clung to him and helped him in his hour of need. This Harold never forgot. He loved his mother with all the strength of his steady heart. Her daughters were married, and provided with cares of their own, and Harold well knew the loneliness of the patient little woman when *he* was not with her.

So he wrote a hasty line of excuse to Mrs. Craven and with a heavy heart boarded the Michigan Central, sorry for those he was leaving behind and for those he was going to meet.

Mrs. Craven's dinner was less lively than usual. Major Craven had insisted on inviting two "pork kings," who could talk of nothing else but pork. And Harold was absent, so was Alice, to whom her hostess had said kindly as they returned from their drive: "I daresay, dear, you would rather lie down and rest, or get into your dressing gown and read a novel, than put on evening costume and sit down to dinner."

"Yes, I should greatly prefer it. I want to write to Mrs. Williams, too. I did not send her a letter yesterday, and I rarely miss doing so on Wednesday. I know she always looks for one."

Alice stayed very contentedly in her room. She pondered long and deeply on all Mrs. Craven had said, and wished that she could please every one by marrying Nevin. Why did

she not love him ? If she dared speak to Mr.
Neale about it ! She blushed at the idea.

Major Craven, who had always been friendly
to his wife's quiet little protegée, inquired the
reason of her absence, and expressed a hope
that all was going on well between her and
Wilfred.

"Oh, as well as can be expected," returned
his wife, laughing. "She is a good little simpleton, and not too ready to take up an idea."

"I don't find her dull by any means," said
Major Craven. "It is quite a relief to meet
any one who does not aim at talking epigrams.
Now I must bid you good-night, Mrs. Wainwright, if I may not escort you home."

The company had by this time departed, all
save Mrs. Wainwright, who remained alone
with her hostess.

"Craven is a good fellow, Mary," said Mrs.
Wainwright. "You are a lucky woman."

"I daresay I am.- Now let me talk to you.
I want to hear what Wilfred said yesterday.
I hope you scolded him for his folly, his rash-
ness."

"Your brother certainly came to pour his
sorrows into my sympathizing bosom," said
Mrs. Wainwright. "But I confess my warmest sympathy has been excited by his being
obliged to marry such a mummy. She will

bore him to death. But there, it seems if he
does not marry her he may starve to death. It
is a desperate alternative."

"My dear, you did not set him against my
poor, rich protegée? He is rather infatuated
about you, but that is, you know, of no use."

"I regret to say it *is* of no use, for I find
your brother very nice and most amusing.
What an idiot Miss Ashland is to refuse him!"

"Yes. I fancied it would have been a case
of 'I came—I saw—I conquered' with Wilfred
and Alice Ashland. I cannot understand her
indifference."

"Well, I think I do," remarked Mrs. Wainwright, dryly, as she arranged the flowers that
adorned her dress.

"You do! Why, what do you mean? What
are you hinting at?" cried Mrs. Craven,
eagerly.

"I think, Mary, that you are quite as foolish
and a good deal blinder than your brother.
Alice Ashland does not care for Wilfred because she has already fallen in love with that
interesting companion of your childhood."

"You cannot believe such an absurdity,"
cried Mrs. Craven, flushing from throat to brow.
"Why, I never thought of such a thing."

"That I quite believe," significantly. "I
am a quiet, indolent creature; I let others do

the talking, but I *see* a great deal. Your brother has been taken up with *me*, you have been taken up with your *farouche* friend, and I have watched you all.''

'' And what have you seen? '' asked Mrs. Craven in a low tone, keeping her eyes carefully cast down.

'' I have seen Miss Ashland's face; and whenever Mr. Neale appears it lights up in the most wonderful way. I don't think the little fool is the least conscious of her own feelings; I protest she warms up into absolute prettiness as soon as he comes. Now she distrusts Wilfred; she is half afraid of him.''

'' But how preposterous of her to throw away her pale fancies on Harold Neale, who scarcely notices her.''

'' Ah! are you sure he does not? My impression is, that not a look, not a word of hers escapes him.''

'' Come, come, this is more than observation; it is creative power.''

Mrs. Wainwright shook her head. '' Your friend has very expressive eyes, as I daresay you know, and they have told me more than he imagines. I am disposed to think he is considerably further gone than she is.''

'' It is impossible,'' said Mrs. Craven, in a low, deep tone.

"Oh, if you like to think so. Just look back over the past month. How much more he has been at your house since Alice Ashland went into training under your supervision. Remember our trips to the World's Fair. Neale had many a good half-hour's practical tete-a-tete with her there; indeed, it might have been longer at Lincoln Park had I not sent Mr. Nevin to break it up."

"I do not think Harold would try to cut out Wilfred."

"Perhaps. But once a man is in love, I should not give much for his good resolutions."

"Really, dear, you don't seem to think there is such a thing as principle."

"Oh, yes, I do; but I suppose he is no stronger than his neighbors. *You* know all about that, no doubt, much better than any one else."

"There is some difference between a man and a boy. At any rate, Harold is far away, or will be far away to-morrow. He has been re-called to Peekskill by his mother's illness."

"Well, keep him at a distance," said Mrs. Wainwright, rising; "it will be better for all parties. I must leave you now. I promised to call for Mr. Smith and take him to Mrs. Potter's reception."

"I hope affairs are progressing smoothly between you and the great 'Kangaroo'?"

"Yes, satisfactorily; so much so that I regret bestowing that very appropriate nickname. Good-night, Mary; are you going to bed like a sober citizen?"

"I am. This worry about Wilfred has upset me."

They exchanged adieus, and the observant Mrs. Wainwright went down to her carriage.

Mrs. Craven sat and studied everything she had heard. Had she been so fooled and blinded as to rejoice in the frequent lingering visits which were due to another's attractions? The more she strove to reject the idea, the more corroborative trifles rose in her memory to indorse Mrs. Wainwright's revolting suspicions.

It was bitter, very bitter, to the proud, passionate woman who best knew what advances she had made to a man who, she began reluctantly to believe, was shielded by that strongest armor, affection for another. It was all too evident. She did not know till now how he had absorbed her. She meant no harm, she told herself; yet she never for an instant regretted her own heartless conduct. To see Harold once more at her feet, to tell him she loved him and bid him leave her forever, this would be joy!

Ah, well! there was no use thinking about it. What needed her whole force of mind and resolution was to accomplish her brother's marriage to Alice Ashland.

"She shall be his wife within a month," she muttered, rising from the cushions where she had writhed in impotent rage. " She shall be safely out of Neale's reach long before they meet again."

She turned to her writing-table, drew a chair, and after a moment's thought wrote a carefully worded letter to Harold Neale—a charming, sympathetic epistle, which the major might have read with perfect impunity.

She thought how she might best charge her communication with the venom which disturbed her own mind. She described the rapid growth of mutual love between Wilfred and Alice, and concluded her letter with a kindly message from her brother, which would convey the impression that he was at her elbow. And then, completely restored to composure, Mrs. Craven extinguished her light and fell asleep.

Alice Ashland longed to solace her depressed spirit by writing a full and true history of the trial through which she had passed to Mrs. Williams, but she had the impression that it would be disloyal to Mrs. Craven and Wilfred if she told the story of her rejection of the latter. New needs had sprung up. She could not go back to the bare existence she had led before she met Nevin and his sister. Her tastes were quiet enough, but her eyes had been opened, and, warmly as she loved Mrs. Williams, she felt that life would indeed be dreary had she no other companionship.

Mrs. Craven saw with much satisfaction the pale, pensive face of her young friend grow paler and sadder. She took no notice of the remarkable fact that for four days Harold had not appeared. This silence was, in Mrs. Craven's opinion, a bad symptom, and she determined to break it by a bold and masterly stroke.

"I forgot to tell you that Mr. Neale has been summoned away—his mother is dangerously ill," said Mrs. Craven to Alice, as they sat together in the drawing-room.

"I am very sorry," exclaimed Alice, laying down *Harper's*. "He is very fond of his mother."

"I did not think you knew he had a mother," said Mrs. Craven, sharply.

"He has spoken of her to me sometimes," said Alice, innocently, quite unembarrassed.

"She is a charming lady. I was going to say

'old lady,' but she is so youthful in appearance. I like Harold very much, too. He used
to be such a good fellow, but I was not quite
pleased with him the other day."

"Indeed." ·

There was no curiosity in the tone.

"No," continued Mrs. Craven. "I thought
him too manly for that sort of self-conceit.
Perhaps I ought not to tell you." She paused,
and Alice looked at her in great surprise.

"We were talking of his leaving Chicago,"
she resumed, and he said, with his grave smile :
'On one account I shall not be sorry to leave ;
your little friend shows her flattering preference for me in a most unmistakable manner.
It would really be touching were it not so
funny, and I am not disposed to fall in love in
return.' "

There was a moment's silence. The color
rose slowly to Alice's cheeks, as if shame and
mortification were penetrating her soul. Though
she did not dream of doubting Mrs. Craven, she
half unconsciously exclaimed :

"He could not have said that."

"Oh, if you imagine I invented the amiable
speech, why—"

"No, no, I do not ; but it seems impossible.
I found him so kind and—sensible. I did like

him and like to talk to him, but I am not in love with him."

"I should be sorry if you were," said Mrs. Craven, with emphasis.

"Indeed—indeed I am not. I am more grieved than I can say to think Mr. Neale could speak of me in such a way. It is unworthy of him."

"So I think, and so I told him," said Mrs. Craven.

"Are you quite sure he meant *me?*" persisted Alice.

"My dear, who else could he mean? I did expect better things from Harold Neale, but it seems he is no better than the rest. My brother would never talk of a woman in that strain. Though it is rather a breach of confidence, I am almost tempted to show you two letters he has written me since you banished him."

"Perhaps Mr. Nevin might not like me to see them," said Alice, shrinking back from the cruel blow just dealt her.

"He need never know. Do read them, Alice. I should like you to see the sort of nature you have rejected."

Alice read the effusions, which were admirably composed, full of veiled sadness, tender and passionate and touching in their entreaties to his sister not to withdraw her friendship and protection from the little darling who seemed to have no one to care for and watch over her. Alice folded them up and returned them to Mrs. Craven with trembling hands and quivering lips.

"He is too good. I do not desire that he should think so much of me. I feel quite angry with myself for not loving him. But I am very young, Mrs. Craven; need I marry any one just yet? I don't feel as if I were fit to be any man's companion."

"My dear Alice, were you any one else I should accuse you of mock modesty."

"No, I am not so modest as you fancy. I want to learn so much to be at all equal to you and Mrs. Wainwright and—Mr. Nevin." Harold's name came to her lips, but she curbed herself in time. "I cannot even know how to behave myself or — or Mr. Neale would never have spoken so cruelly of me," and she burst into a passionate flood of tears.

"Alice, dear child," cried Mrs. Craven, delighted at the success of her scheme, yet not unmoved by the sight of her distress, "you take a mere trifle far too much to heart. The boasting of a man like Harold Neale, who really knows nothing of society, is not worth a moment's thought. I saw nothing whatever to remark in your conduct. I love your candor and simplicity. Go bathe your eyes and let us drive to the Fair. Trust me, my dear, I will always be your friend."

Alice's heart thrilled with warmest gratitude as she pressed her trembling lips to the soft, smiling mouth of the beautiful superior being who deigned to love her.

But even Mrs. Craven's boundless condescension could not console her.

Moreover, she recognized, with a keen sense of degradation, that Harold was right. She loved him, and her ideal was shattered. She must forget her own folly and try to be worthy of the friendship so generously bestowed on her. Indeed, she was almost disposed to think she ought to marry Wilfred Nevin out of gratitude to his sister.

"Alice is already disposed to regard you with a sort of grateful kindness which will lead her further. I suspect Neale has been—knowingly or not—a bit of a traitor. Be ready to start for Chicago on receipt of a message from me. Keep out of Neale's way. Your letters do you credit; continue them. And let me have the guardian's address—I mean Bond; I may want to see him."

So wrote Mary Craven to her brother.

"Could you not steal a march on your schem-
ing sister and come up secretly for a couple of
days? I feel as if a long talk with you would
do me good, for shortly the ' Kangaroo ' will
have me forever, except now and again, of
course."

So wrote the charming Mrs. Wainwright to
the exiled lover.

CHAPTER VII.

WHEN Harold Neale reached Peekskill he
found his mother in a critical condition, but
slightly better. The doctor in attendance had
wrestled with the disease successfully, but in
her weak state feared a relapse. It was not
until she had been carefully prepared that the
sufferer was allowed to see her son. His
mother could only smile faintly as Harold bent
over her and took her thin, nearly transparent
hand in his with infinite tenderness. He could
not for a few moments trust his voice. He
knew the loneliness of her life. She could never
open her heart to any of her children, except
to Harold, the strongest and most combative
of them all. Between the mother and son
there was profound sympathy, and the dream

of Harold's maturer manhood was to make the
evening of her days peaceful, bright and full of
affection and warmth. With his father, Harold had little in common. Mr. Neale, Sr., was
narrow and domineering, and years of rheuma-
tism were beginning to enfeeble him, and make
his stern and once equable temper irritable, at
times querulous.

From the time her son returned Mrs. Neale
began slowly, very slowly, to gain strength;
but for several weeks she required the utmost
care. Her son's daily visits and quiet talk
comforted and supported the mother.

With all his tender care for, and anxiety
about, his mother, Harold's thoughts often
strayed to the drama he knew was being en-
acted in Chicago. The honest preference Alice
had shown for him had completed the charm
she exercised. It would be a delicious occupation to win the full, womanly love of this delicate creature, whose gentleness was not weak,
whose ignorance was not dull. What a contrast to his first stormy love affair and to some
slighter experiences through which he had since
passed! Her wealth was a hindrance. What
had he to offer that could in any way balance
it? He was pondering these things with more
than usual bitterness, because his anxiety about
his mother had been somewhat relieved.

While he was thus meditating one of the men of the farm came to tell him that a gentleman at the house wished to see him, and to his surprise he found Major Craven.

"Surprised to see me, eh?" said the major, shaking hands cordially. "Chicago got too hot and dusty for me, and I got tired of the great Fair, but Mrs. Craven means to see it out; I am a great deal more comfortable on the Hudson, anyhow."

Harold rather liked Major Craven, and by no means envied him the possession of his peerless wife. After a long and rambling talk, he reverted again to his wife. "I never knew Mrs. Craven stay so long in either Chicago or New York, she generally wants to quit earlier; but she is on another tack now," he nodded knowingly. "Of course you are in the secret! It's her anxiety about her brother that is keeping her. You know what a slippery fellow Nevin is. He has given Mrs. Craven lots of trouble. It's quite natural she should try and secure that heiress she has picked up for him; nice little girl—too good for Wilfred, I think."

Harold murmured an inarticulate assent.

"Yes; it has given Mrs. Craven a lot of trouble. She doesn't think I know it, but I do!" he chuckled. "She is far too spunky to confess herself beaten if she can help it, and so

I say nothing; but I'm pretty sure Wilfred was refused. I suspect my precious brother-in-law, though, is much more cut up about Mrs. Wainwright's engagement to old Smith, which has just been announced."

"Has it?" cried Harold, with vivid interest, his heart beating quickly at the dim, delightful possibility suggested by Craven's revelations.

"Ay! it is a good thing; it will be diamond cut diamond with them; but the poor little Californian, Alice Ashland, that is a different matter. However, I can't interfere. I'm quite sure my wife is biding her time; she'll bring up her man to the scratch again. She holds on like grim death to anything she takes up. You used to be chums in your boy-and-girl days, she tells me, and she is one who never forgets old times. I can tell you, you are a prime favorite still."

After the major left Harold went to sit a while with his mother, as was his wont in the afternoon, but he scarce knew what he talked about. That Nevin had been refused was more than he expected. He did not anticipate such decision on Alice's part.

It was by an effort he brought his thoughts under control, and compelled himself to show his usual care in trying to amuse and interest the invalid.

She was surprised and pleased to hear of the major's visit. The little description of Major Craven's appearance and its results excited and fatigued her. Harold, therefore, seeing she was inclined to sleep, left her earlier than he usually did, and calling his favorite dog, set forth on a solitary ramble, to commune with his own heart, to search out his spirit, and strive to come to some conclusion respecting his future line of conduct.

As he pressed up the side of the historic Catskills with firm, elastic tread, his spirits rose, his purpose disengaged itself from the mist of doubt and depression which had blurred it, and at length, reaching a shady nook, where many a time in bygone days he had secluded himself to plan his future, or to think of beautiful Mary Nevin, he lay down, and the dog sat gravely beside him with an air of alertness, as if determined to keep watch while his master slept or rested.

But sleep and dreams were far from Harold's brain. His thoughts began to take order. If Nevin had tried his hand and failed, one barrier to his own progress was removed. Why should he not do his best to win what he so ardently desired ? How was it that he had so quickly grown to love this quiet, half-developed girl ? Only his heart answered : "I love her."

What a restful home such a woman could make! And this defenseless creature was at the mercy of mere intriguers, reckless of her happiness. It was the duty of any disinterested friend to rescue her if possible.

"She liked me better than any of the rest—I think she did ; but I ought not to be too sure. I am half inclined to try my luck. If I fail, she would be no worse off than she is now. If she cares for me, I could make her happy in her own way. I wish she hadn't that pot of money. I'd rather she hadn't a rap ; it would only make me more eager to marry her! Then she is so lonely, so unprotected! Old Mrs. Williams is a fine old woman, but no companion for Alice. How desolate she is ! I must make my father come to a definite arrangement. ' The laborer is worthy of his hire.' "

Then the regular sequence of thought became confused with sweet, glowing visions of perfect understanding, of rest and security, of gentle caresses. Yes, as soon as his mother was a little stronger he would return to Chicago and risk an avowal of his hopes and fears. When could he start ? His mother was distinctly out of danger, and his sister could stay a couple of weeks longer. Yes, he would tell his mother that a matter of vital importance required his presence in Chicago, and she would let him go.

Soon he hoped to return with news that would comfort and cheer her.

So, in a restless but hopeful mood, Harold Neale rose up, a clear purpose once more steadying his will, and walked home less rapidly than he had set forth.

At the entrance he met his sister with a letter in her hand. "Oh, Harold, I have been looking everywhere for you. I have just heard from Walter " (her husband). " His uncle is going back to Texas, and has wired us to say he is coming to-morrow for a week just to bid us good-by, and I must be at home to do the honors, for you know he is a very important personage to us, and really, mother would rather have you than any of us."

"But wait a bit, Annie. I want very much to go to Chicago."

"I am really very sorry, Harold, but I cannot stay. I have ordered Tod to bring round the buggy ; I can just catch the 5:20 and reach home about nine."

Harold was fairly caught. Destiny was too strong for him. He could not leave his mother, and his sister's absence was prolonged. Meantime letters of tender inquiry from Mrs. Craven, both to Harold and the invalid, came frequently, but with rare mention of Alice. Yet Harold could make out that she was still residing with

her fascinating protectress. At last his sister
returned to take her place beside the delicate
mother, and the same day Harold Neale set
out for Chicago.

Mrs. Craven was growing cross and impa-
tient ; she was tired of the Windy City and its
"greatest show on earth." She had several
tempting invitations to join some friends at
Newport and one still more attractive within
a dozen miles of Peekskill. "If only Alice
could make up her mind to marry Wilfred and
have done with it."

Still she kept a fair face and watched un-
ceasingly for the right moment at which Nevin
might reappear.

Alice was very still and humble, looking and
feeling miserable. She had learned enough of
Ward McAllister's world to know that Mrs.
Craven would be leaving Chicago, and still
nothing was said about Alice accompany-
ing her.

"I ought to prepare for returning home,
dear Mrs. Craven," said Alice, timidly, one
morning when the servants had left the room.

"Not yet, Alice. I shall be leaving Chicago
for a few weeks and I need not say how much I
need you to stay with me. Besides—but I don't
like to talk of future plans just yet. Tell me,

dear, would it annoy you if Wilfred were to come here ? I want very much to see him. He writes to say he wants to go to Mexico, or any- where out of the States "—with a sigh; "and you need not mind, for he has resolved to be your friend, if he can be no more."

"Of course I cannot expect to banish your brother, and I am very grateful to him for wishing to be my friend," said Alice, coloring and looking embarrassed. "But the studio will soon be closed, and then I think I ought to return to my old home and poor Mrs. Williams. You have taught me much and done me a great deal of good."

"Poor, dear child," said Mrs. Craven, "how frightfully dull it will be for you!"

"I never used to be dull at Santa Cruz," re- turned Alice, thoughtfully; "yet somehow I feel as if I should be now."

"You must not stay there long," said Mrs. Craven. "When do you say your studio closes?"

"On the 19th."

"Why, that is only two weeks off," and Mrs. Craven was silent for a few minutes; then apologizing for leaving Alice, she soon after went out.

Alice was accustomed to be left alone of late; she did not in the least resent Mrs. Craven's desertion; she accepted it as unavoidable, but it depressed her with the sense of being of no importance to any one. Moreover, that terrible speech of Neale's, as reported to her, had destroyed her self-reliance. If her conduct was such as to create so false an impression, the less she saw of strangers and society the better. A feeling of gratitude toward Nevin began to develop in her heart, though she did not wish to see him, for she had never felt quite at ease with him.

She had been full of these thoughts as she walked back after her morning's work, a couple of days after the above conversation, and rang the door-bell almost mechanically.

"Mrs. Craven is in the drawing-room, ma'am," said the servant, waving her hand invitingly in that direction.

Alice, taking it for granted that her hostess wished to speak to her, walked into the room, but instead of Mrs. Craven she found a gentleman reading a newspaper. At the sound of the opening door he threw it aside and started to his feet. It was Wilfred Nevin.

Alice could scarcely resist the desperate inclination to run away; she was startled, ashamed, disposed to cry. Nevin looked ill, too, and less debonair than usual. He hastened to put her at her ease.

"I am inclined to apologize for being here, Miss Ashland," he said, pressing her hand for a moment. "I really did not think there was any chance of our meeting this morning," and he smiled pleasantly. "As it *has* so happened, may I speak frankly--may I beg you to let bygones be bygones? Allow me the privilege of friendship during the short time I shall be in America. It would make my last days with my sister so much brighter." He paused suddenly, as if in great emotion.

"You are very kind," cried Alice, delighted with the proposition. "I shall be so glad to have you for a friend. It is more than I could expect that you should care for my friendship."

"You know how much I cared," began Nevin, but checking himself. "We are not to revert to bygones. Tell me, how are your studies progressing? I expect to see great things. I assure you I often wished you could have seen the Catskills or the Palisades on the Hudson. I was always finding subjects for sketches ; indeed, I was almost tempted to try my own hand," etc., etc.

And Alice, a good deal to her surprise, found herself launched into an easy conversation on art and scenery with the man she shrank from meeting three short hours ago.

"Why, Alice," cried Mrs. Craven, coming in

quickly, "I had no idea you were here." She spoke in a tone of surprise.

A little pleasant chat ensued, then Nevin said he had promised to call on some friends and rose to go.

"Come back to dinner," said his sister, "and be sure you do nothing rash—nothing at all, indeed, until you consult me."

Nevin laughed, bowed to Alice and withdrew.

"He is looking wretchedly ill, isn't he?" said Mrs. Craven, turning to Alice. "Poor fellow, I am so glad you have got your meeting over in this *accidental* way; it would be foolish not to be good friends; indeed, there is no reason why you should not."

Nevin's return appeared to break the spell of undefined discomfort that had oppressed both Alice and her hostess. He made himself a pleasant, unobtrusive companion. He talked of his future life in remote regions and expressed a manly regret for his wasted youth, his lost opportunities. Alice began to feel like an indulgent sister to a prodigal but penitent brother.

Mr. Robert Bond was busy as usual over his papers and accounts one sultry morning. He wore a look of satisfaction; a fresh victim had just effected a loan through his "agency," as he termed it, and he had been calculating his immediate and prospective gains. In this agreeable occupation he was roused by the entrance of his shock-headed boy, who placed a note before his master, and said, interrogatively : "See her ? "

Mr. Bond shoved his glasses a little nearer his eyes, opened the note and read : "Can you speak to Mrs. Craven for a few minutes ?"

"O Lord !" ejaculated Bond, in a low tone, hastily folding up the note again. "Ay, let her come in—let her come in."

He started up and pushed away his chair, and was half-way across the room when his visitor entered.

What an apparition of loveliness for his sordid chamber! A very perfect costume of silvery-gray satin and grenadine and shiny gray beads ; a bonnet, also gray, with downy soft feathers, tipped with silver, in the Mesdames McCrae's best style ; gloves and shoes and parasol all delicately matching, lent to and borrowed from the wearer additional beauty. Even old Bond was impressed and hesitated how to address this dazzling vision.

With a half-surprised, half-contemptuous glance Mrs. Craven took in the details of the room and recognized the effect she produced on the owner.

"Do you know who I am?" she asked, showing her white teeth with a frank, amused smile.

"I think I do, I think I do, ma'am; my lady, you are Mr. Nevin's sister; let me give you a chair."

"I want to talk to you about my brother and your ward," said Mrs. Craven, seating herself.

"I am sure, ma'am, I'm all attention. It's a long time since I heard anything of them; and, indeed, I did not think your brother was the sort of man to let the grass grow under his feet."

"On the contrary, his precipitancy has nearly ruined all our plans. I say 'our,' Mr. Bond, for, though I have not the pleasure of knowing you, I know all your plans and the bargain you made with my brother."

"Eh! do you know?" grinning confusedly, and pressing the nib of a pen on a rather black thumb-nail. "Well, I *did* think that little—a —agreement was to be a secret between Mr. Nevin and myself, of course."

"Of course," interrupted Mrs. Craven. "It was quite right and natural that he should confide the whole affair to *me*, especially as neither of you could have carried out your scheme

without my help. It is equally natural that
you should look after your own interests,
though straitlaced people might say the means
you took to secure them were not exactly creditable."

"Well, you see, as my friend Teddy says,
what people say of me doesn't reach my
ears," returned Bond, with a deprecatory
writhe, rubbing his hands together. "And
how is Mr. Nevin getting on, may I be so bold
as to ask?"

"He is not getting on at all," cried Mrs.
Craven, with a burst. "He is such an impa-
tient creature, and your ward is an obstinate
simpleton. He proposed too soon, and she refused him."

"Great Scott! think of that now. Such a
fine, elegant gentleman. I didn't think any
young lady would say him nay," and Bond
began nervously to gather up the papers which
lay about and sort them in an unconscious
way. "And do you mean to say they cannot
agree?"

"I intend that they shall agree," said Mrs.
Craven, closing her mouth firmly.

"Then, what do you mean to do, my lady—I
mean ma'am?" asked Bond, again nibbling the
top of his pen.

"Listen. I have not much time to spend

here, and if you intend to get your money you *must* help me. I suspect that Miss Ashland has taken a fancy to a very unsuitable person, whom she unfortunately met at my residence, and one who would not lose an atom of his just rights to save your life. He would be more likely to expose what he considered a fraud than lend himself to any little arrangement that might facilitate matters. In short, he must *not* interfere with my brother."

" No, certainly not ; that's right."

Mrs. Craven's eyes rested with unspeakable disdain on the withered, ignoble face opposite her.

"I'm sure you have only to command me," added Bond.

" I have managed to bring my brother and Miss Ashland together again, and she is playing at friendship with him. Let them pursue that game for a while, then you must strike a blow and cut off her retreat. Your sister is her companion ? "

" She is."

" And I presume you have a good deal of influence on Mrs.—"

" Williams," put in Bond. " Yes," rubbing his hands softly, " I *rather* think I have."

" Then you must make her give up her engagement with Miss Ashland. Invent some-

thing imperative ; rent that cottage at Santa
Cruz or sell it ; cut off her supports, leave her
no ' stand-by ' but Mr. Nevin. She is peculiarly
desolate ; this ought to make her thank her
stars that she has found such a protector as my
brother."

"My sister will no doubt do as I bid her,"
said Bond, laying down his pen. " But it seems
a little strange to me that you should be so
desperately anxious to get my ward for your
brother. Grand people like you might have a
choice of heiresses, I should think."

" Heiresses fenced round with bristling
hedges of relatives, well up as Joseph Bulfinch
in the private history of every man in society,
and cousins anxious to keep the money in
the family. Do not waste my time and your
own in idle conjecture. Will you follow my
suggestion, or shall we break off negotiations
and send your ward back to the wilds
from which you dragged her, poor child ! for
your own ends ? "

"I don't pretend to be an angel no more
than Mr. Nevin does, but I thought, and I still
think, I was doing the best I could for Miss
Ashland by pushing her marriage. I'm of your
opinion, that this shilly-shallying ought to be
put a stop to ; but you are as quick as a flash of
lightning and down on a man before he knows

where he is. I think your idea is very good, very good, and you'll see I'll not be long in acting on it. I'll get Mrs. Williams off to Puget Sound and give her permanent employment among the *clams*. But I hope when the knot is tied hard and fast Mr. Nevin will not object to a little annuity in consideration of the help she is giving him."

"She is helping you, too, Mr. Bond," said Mrs. Craven, shrewdly, "and I hope *you* will not prove ungrateful." She rose as she spoke. "We understand each other, then," she continued. "Our interests are alike. I suppose I may depend on you?"

"I'll be as true as the needle to the pole," cried Bond, enthusiastically.

Mrs. Craven laughed as, with a slight nod of her head, she left the room.

"Well, I've seen a few clippers in my life, but she 'takes the cake,' as they say; regular fire and tow! There's something more than her anxiety about her brother under it all. As to my sister, she dare not refuse me anything. I must send her to Clallam or some other hole in the Northwest."

Meanwhile, Mrs. Craven drove off down State Street, and her carriage was obliged to stop near "Serjel Coopers," on account of a block. As she looked listlessly at the passers-by she suddenly recognized Harold Neale, coming from the "L" road. She waved her hand and caught his eye. He came readily enough, and the next instant she was exclaiming, with smiling lips:

"Back again in Chicago, Mr. Neale! What on earth has brought you here?"

CHAPTER VIII.

"My mother is considerably better and out of danger, and I have some important business to attend to here," replied Harold, shaking her hand.

"Shall you be long in Chicago?" she asked.

"Only a day or two."

"We are, unfortunately, going out to dinner to-day, but can you look in and have a cup of tea a little before four?"

"Certainly, I shall be most happy," returned Harold, his eyes lighting up with joy.

"Do not be late." She kissed her hand to him as she stepped back and signed to the driver that he might go on.

"He is not handsome," thought Mrs. Craven, "but how much better looking than most handsome men. Oh, no one ever loved me as

Harold did. and I treated him abominably. I think he likes me a little still."

Then the horrible suspicion flashed across her brain: Could the light that came to his eyes have been evoked by the prospect of meeting Alice Ashland? No, impossible! Mrs. Wainwright was dreaming; yet "He shall not see her" was her fixed determination, as she alighted within a short distance of her own door and dismissed the conveyance.

"Has Mr. Nevin been here this morning?" asked Mrs. Craven, as she entered the house.

"No, ma'am," said the butler.

"Then send to the Auditorium and say I want to speak to him at once; if Mr. Nevin is not there, let him be found."

"Very well, ma'am."

Mrs. Craven went to her room.

At lunch Major Craven, who had also returned from the East, joined his wife and Miss Ashland.

"I have written to Mrs. Williams and Mr. Watts," said Alice, "telling them that the studio would be closed next week, and that you cannot stay in Chicago much longer, therefore I had better return home."

"Well, dear, I wish you had spoken to me before you wrote. I shall not leave Chicago before the end of next month, and though I cannot exactly fix my plans, there is time enough; you need not be in such a hurry to run away from us."

"No, let us all go back to my place on the Hudson together. You don't want to go to Newport this year, Mary?" said Major Craven.

"I shall not commit myself," she returned, laughing. Nevin preserved an expressive silence, his eyes fixed on his plate.

"I do not wish to go, indeed I do not," said Alice, earnestly. "You are all so good to me, but I fear to be in your way, and I do not want to desert my own home."

"And we are, of course, tired of so tiresome and naughty a little girl," said Mrs. Craven, with a pleasant smile. "However, things will arrange themselves. I was going to propose, as it is such a fine day, to drive to Lincoln Park; unfortunately, I have had a manifesto from Mme. Abbott, who is coming to try on my fall costumes and plan an evening dress or two, and if I lose this chance I may not catch her again, for Abbott is a personage, I assure you."

"I am very sorry," cried Alice, impulsively.

"Never mind, Miss Ashland; I'm a capital whip, and will drive you carefully. What do you say?" said Nevin.

"An excellent suggestion," exclaimed Mrs. Craven. "Will you accept it, Alice?"

"Yes; thank you very much."

"Then I will order the buggy to come round at three, and you'll have a nice long afternoon. Ring the bell, Wilfred."

"Ha! Nevin, you haven't served your apprenticeship to drawing-room life for nothing!" said Major Craven, significantly.

His wife looked at him with a warning frown.

The major rose soon after and left the room, saying he was going to the Hawthorne races.

Mrs. Craven soon followed his example and Alice went to get herself ready.

"I must steer with caution," thought Harold Neale, as he rang the bell at the Craven residence and was admitted into the cool, perfumed hall.

"This way, sir," said the butler, ushering him upstairs to a small room where Mrs. Craven sat in softened light amid a profusion of delicious flowers, fresh from a second toilet.

"Bring the tea; and, Christina, I am not at home."

The girl bowed obedience and retired.

"I'm quite glad to hear all about your mother and dear old Peekskill," said Mrs. Craven. "I hope your mother improves?"

"Very slowly. Yet she does improve. I doubt, however, if she will be able to stand the winter, though we have the most sheltered spot on the Hudson. I think I shall take her to California."

" It must be a great comfort for her having you at home," returned Mrs. Craven, and she continued to speak of their mutual experiences in the past, approaching dexterously the scene of their stormy parting, with the intention both of eliciting some expression of his feelings from Harold and of giving her own explanation of the fact that she threw him over for a wealthy suitor.

But her skill was unavailing. Harold's eyes wandered nervously with an expectant look to the door, by which he supposed every moment Alice would appear.

" Are you not a little *distrait*, Mr. Neale ? " she asked, with a well-got-up air of playfulness. " Who are you looking for—Wilfred or Miss Ashland ? "

" I rather expected to find Miss Ashland with you," said Harold, with such unhesitating frankness that Mrs. Craven was a little reassured. " Wilfred is not in Chicago, I heard."

" Yes, he *was* away," said Mrs. Craven, slowly, for she was making up her mind for a big, bold lie. " But he came back about a week ago, and I am sure you will be glad to hear that my hopes have been fulfilled. Miss Ashland and Wilfred are engaged ; and he has driven her to Lincoln Park to-day. I am sure Wilfred will be a very devoted husband, as he ought to be, for she sincerely loves him."

Silence. It was a most unexpected blow, and for a moment Harold was stunned. He rallied himself by an effort.

"I congratulate you," he said, looking down. "I hope Nevin will do her justice. Miss Ashland seems to me something of a home bird."

"Like other women, she will probably become what her circumstances make her," said Mrs. Craven, shortly. "As the engagement is only just made, I beg you will not speak of it at present to any one."

"Certainly not, if you desire it."

"I am going back to the Hudson," continued Mrs. Craven, wishing to avoid the subject, "to refresh myself with a glimpse of the dear old Catskills."

"Indeed ! It is long since you were there. New York has claimed you since your marriage."

"Yes ; but I long to see the old spot. Shall you be at home in October ? "

"I suppose so."

"Then you must be my guide, philosopher and

friend in the scenes of my youth," said Mrs.
Craven, stealing a watchful glance at his som-
ber countenance.

"I am, of course, at your service."

"If you are disengaged to-morrow," said
Mrs. Craven, as he rose to go, "come to dinner and meet the affianced ones." She told
herself: "He will not come."

"If I settle my business to-morrow morning
I am bound to catch the night mail home,"
said Harold. "Should I not see you before I
go, pray congratulate Wilfred for me at the
right moment. Good-by."

"He came here to seek her. Wainwright is
right, for once. How gallantly he took it.
How his eyes sought that door. Oh, how different he is from the willow-wands of men
that surround me!" So soliloquized Mrs.
Craven as she stood looking after Harold
Neale for a minute, with her brows knit and a
look of victory and love written on her beautiful face. Mrs. Craven was not surprised to
receive a line from Neale: "He found it necessary to return home immediately."

"I wonder what real business he had in Chicago," she thought. "At any rate, he is safe
out of the way. When he meets Alice again
she shall be Mrs. Wilfred Nevin."

Another week had nearly passed and Alice

had had no answer from Mrs. Williams. Mr. Watts had paid her a visit and stayed to luncheon, where he seemed anything but comfortable. On Friday morning, however, she received two terrible letters. One from Mr. Bond, saying that he and Mr. Watts had accepted a very good offer for the Santa Cruz cottage and let it on lease.

The other was from poor Mrs. Williams, and was an incoherent production ; something about a broken heart at having to leave Santa Cruz and her dear Alice, praying God to bless her and restore them to each other.

Besides the letter a scrap of paper had been thrust into the envelope, on which were the words : "I can't help myself, dear ; I can't, indeed. I'll tell you all yet ; wait a bit, and *burn* this."

Alice read both letters before she grasped the situation. Without a home, a tie, a claim on any one, what was to become of her ? Where was she to turn ?

There was a tinge of mystery, too, in this sudden wrenching asunder of Mrs. Williams and herself that completed her distress.

Bond was at the bottom of it. She had an innate distrust of Bond. Mr. Watts, though so much nicer, was a mere puppet in his hands.

Alice sat down, hoping Mrs. Craven might

come in before going out, as she often did in the forenoon.   Once more she read Mr. Bond's letter, thinking all the time she heard his thin, harsh voice uttering the smooth sentences, and almost seeing his sycophantic grin.   Her pulse beat quick with an indignant sense of helplessness.   Why did they tear Mrs. Williams from her, and why, oh! why did not Mrs. Craven come?

As she thought, the handle of the door turned.   At the sound Alice started up and went forward so eagerly that she nearly rushed into Nevin's arms as he came in.   She was too full of her troubles to be in any way confused.

"Oh, where—where is Mrs. Craven?" she exclaimed, with a genuine ring of distress in her voice.

"She has just gone out," he returned, looking earnestly at her.

"How unfortunate!   I wanted her *so* much," and a great sob rose in her throat, in spite of her brave effort to be calm.

"What has happened?" asked Nevin, with grave sympathy.   "Can I be of any use?"

Alice looked at him for a moment of doubt and then broke out: "No, no; no one can be of any use to me!   Mr. Bond can do what he likes!"

"Old rascal!   What has he been about?"

asked Nevin, with an accent of real wrath that fitted Alice's mood exactly. "I see," he continued, "you have letters. Are they the trouble? Am I presuming too much if I ask to know what distresses you? My sister will not return for an hour or so. It might be a relief to tell me, even *me*," with a grave smile.

"I should be very glad, as you are so good as to care. Read these and you will not wonder at my feeling desolate." She handed him the letters and threw herself on the lounge with self-abandonment very new to her.

Nevin read both epistles in silence, then sat down by her and returned them to her.

"Very hard lines for you," he said. "But I do not see how it is to be helped." (Alice had loyally burned poor Mrs. Williams's private note.)

"Don't you see it takes away from me any shadow of home? When Mrs. Craven goes I shall be quite—quite alone!" cried Alice.

"And Mary has so many engagements," said Nevin, as if to himself, beginning to pace to and fro with a troubled air. "That will not last long, however. You can make a home where you choose."

"I am afraid I cannot! Where can I go? To some strange old lady, who will not like me? For I do not get on with people—I am misunderstood," and she thought of Harold.

"But when they know you they love you!" cried Nevin, and continued his walk in silence till Alice rose, saying:

"Nothing can be done till I see Mrs. Craven."

"Stay—stay for a few minutes, Miss Ashland, I have a solution to propose," said Nevin, with agitation. "Pray hear it patiently." He had thoroughly dramatic instincts and threw himself into his part, be the part what it might.

Alice sat down again. He had so effectively played the calm friend that Alice hardly anticipated what was coming.

"I ought not, perhaps, to revert to my own wishes," he went on—"wishes I have tried to resign, but cannot. Why, Alice, will you not accept a home with me? No, do not speak yet; hear me out." He sat down on the lounge beside her. "I can see plainly enough that you have no love for me. I feel too much for you not to perceive your indifference. But as a friend my society gives you some little pleasure. Do I flatter myself too much?"

"No, indeed!" cried Alice, eager to make some amends for her guilty coldness; "you are always nice and pleasant."

Nevin smiled. "Then do you think it impossible for me to make you happy? Dear Alice (I must call you Alice), you are so deliciously pure and simple you don't know what love is. I will never believe you cared a fig for *any* man." Alice winced. "Let me try and teach you; I know your heart, your mind; I know the sort of life that would suit you; I am not a bad fellow. I am a poor man, I cannot tempt you with wealth, but we shall have enough for a quiet life. If you accept me you can do what you will, independent of guardians or any other nuisance of that kind, and you will make one man very happy."

His quiet earnestness touched Alice. No one else had ever loved her except poor Mrs. Williams, and gratitude alone ought to make her. appreciate a "free-will" offering like Nevin's love. Why should she not accept him; why should she remain friendless any longer?

"Will you at least consider my proposal?" persisted Nevin, humbly, after a long pause.

"You are too good to me," said Alice, softly. "I feel ashamed of not—of not being in love with you. I am greatly surprised that you care about me; I hardly deserve it. You could not like to have a wife who was not in love with you?"

"I should like you to be my wife on any terms," eagerly.

"Afterward you might be very sorry; I'm so different from—"

"That is your greatest charm," he interrupted. "You are so fresh, so unlike the women I have been accustomed to. Listen to me. I have had the offer of an employment in British Columbia. If you will accept me I will give it up. It is not a place I would take *you* to. If you refuse, I will start next week and never—I swear it—never return. My future is in your hands; do with it what you will."

Alice was greatly shaken. Firmly believing all he said, it seemed all but imperative on her to accept him. Who would ever care so much for her again ? and she said tremulously :

"If indeed you think me so necessary to you, if you are satisfied with the sort of feeling I have for you, I think—I think I would try to be very good and careful."

"If!" cried Nevin, interrupting her and catching her hand in both his own. "I make no conditions. I only ask the right of a husband to be with you always, to help you, to teach you to love me. Do you know—can you see the delight even this faint consent gives me ? Make it more, more distinct; give me your promise to be my wife as soon as matters can be arranged."

"Yes," said Alice, slowly, almost solemnly, "I will, and I shall love you when we are married, I am sure I shall." She spoke calmly, without any of the blushing hesitation natural at such a time.

Nevin wisely took his tone from her.

"How can I thank you enough? Even for the sake of this delightful moment, I would not have tried to win your consent if I did not believe I could insure your happiness, dearest."

Alice felt pleased at his earnestness; but she wanted to go away, to think, to relieve her heart by a good cry.

"Must you leave me?" said Nevin, as she made a move as if to go; then he continued: "But I must remember there is some difference in our feelings. I shall see you this evening. Now I have your permission to go and speak to old Bond; he is sure to be in his office early and late. Good-by, my sweet."

He opened the door and left her. Then he went into Mrs. Craven's sitting-room again and his sister immediately followed.

"Well, Mary," he cried, triumphantly, "I'm all right *this* time. She is fully and completely committed."

"I *am* glad!" exclaimed Mrs. Craven. "I

did not think you would strike home so deci-
sively at the first blow. I *am* glad!"

"She is a nice little thing—really, she is! I
was quite pleased with her. But, mind, she is
not one bit in love with me—not an atom—and
it's really better. I hope she won't grow too
desperately fond by and by."

"Nonsense! Now, the sooner we make it
universally known that you *are* engaged, the
better. Let us 'haste to the wedding.' Ah,
Wilfred, 'all's well that ends well.' I must go
to Alice now. Where is she?"

"In her room weeping, I suppose. She ought
to have stayed and let me kiss away her tears."

CHAPTER IX.

MRS. CRAVEN wrote a long letter to Harold
Neale, apologizing for not writing since he had
left Chicago, but she had been so very busy
arranging for Wilfred's wedding, which was to
take place on the 23d of the month, for her own
part she would not be sorry to see the last of
the "billing and cooing of the turtle-doves."
Wilfred talked of inviting him to be best man;
and immediately it was over, she intended to

leave Chicago for Peekskill, and hoped to have a good time at the old spot.

Harold Neale read this epistle over a second time. The perusal justified his anticipations. The letter was cunningly contrived to stab him, and accomplish its end ; but he did not dream it was designed. Her letter seemed to him the natural sequence of her announcement that her brother and Miss Ashland were engaged.

Meanwhile, Mrs. Craven contrived to keep Alice in a constant whirl. She was positively alarmed at the amount of clothes and toilet accessories which her energetic friend declared to be absolutely necessary.

Major Craven enforced his congratulations with the gift of a handsome bracelet, and made much of her in every way.

Nevin was constantly with her, and, for the first two weeks, most judicious. He amused her by planning routes, describing the beauties and wonders he was to show her, and he kept her mind full of himself and his projects. Harold was never mentioned ; indeed, Alice thought she had forgotten him. The guardians were smiling and satisfied. Mrs. Williams wrote in delight, and said she would beg her brother to let her attend the wedding.

All looked fair and promising. Alice was

almost embarrassed by the number of rings and lockets and little costly "charms" to hang to her watch-chain with which Wilfred loaded her.

"I shall never be able to wear them all. Pray do not bring me presents every day," she begged.

"Very well. To hear is to obey. Only, whenever I see anything extra pretty I am seized with an irresistible desire to buy it for you," urged Nevin.

And now the last week of Alice's girlish life had begun; on Wednesday she was to become Mrs. Wilfred Nevin, and at the thought she felt a curious, uneasy creepiness.

The truth was, that Nevin had begun to get a little tired of the part he had hitherto played with such spirit and judgment.

Alice felt rather than perceived the indefinable change; she told herself she was nervous, childish and unreasonable; but a vague, unpleasant impression would grow upon her that Wilfred Nevin, keen, jesting, brightly hard, was a more natural man than the quiet, kindly Nevin, who seemed to understand her thoughts before she uttered them.

"You are not keeping up to the mark, Wilfred," said his sister one evening. "You are allowing the old original Adam to peep out."

" You ought to remember what a desperate drill I have gone through. Is it to be wondered at that I break out at last? Never mind, I am going to buy her *the* ring to-morrow, and I shall be as courteous as a young knight of the troubadour days."

The "to-morrow" broke brightly and softly. Alice had lain long awake, thinking over her quiet past. If the future promised more color and variety, would it be as free from pain?

But the self-commune told upon her, and when Nevin followed her to the drawing-room after luncheon, he asked, tenderly, what had disturbed her, as she looked pale and sad. Of course she assured him she was well and happy, and they talked for a few minutes with renewed confidence on Alice's part.

"I have ventured to bring you yet another ring," he said, at length, drawing a very small parcel from his pocket. "It is as well to ascertain if it is the right size," he added, producing a plain gold ring, and was in the act of trying it on her finger when the butler entered, and, addressing Alice, said :

"There's a gentleman, Miss Ashland, says *his* name is Ashland, asking to see you."

"Ashland!" echoed Alice, amazed. But she had scarcely uttered the word when a very tall man, exceedingly brown and sunburned, with dark hair and eyes, appeared behind the startled butler, and, pushing him aside, strode into the room, stopping short in the middle.

After one comprehensive glance around the room he fixed his piercing eyes on Alice, and asked, in a rough voice: " Are you my cousin, Alice Ashland ? "

" I am Alice Ashland," she returned, rising in her extreme surprise, " but I do not think I have any cousins."

" No, I daresay not," he returned, with a laugh.

"Pray, who are you, sir ? " asked Nevin, haughtily, advancing between Alice and the intruder.

"I am Thomas Ashland, her uncle John's only surviving son," nodding to Alice. " But she never even heard of me, I suppose. Our fathers parted years ago. And you "—sharply —"I suppose you are her lover. I'm glad to make your acquaintance. Shake ! Cousin Alice, I'll come to your wedding as your nearest of kin," and he sat down unasked in one of the brocaded velvet chairs that stood near him.

Nevin looked at him, a smile stealing around his mouth. He was too sure of his own position to be disturbed by the intrusion of any eccentric relative. He would neither be uncivil nor admit his claim.

"Well, my good sir, you cannot expect Miss Ashland to accept you as a relative without something in the way of credentials. Very possibly what you say is correct, but—"

"Ah! I understand. Well, I have left all my papers—that is, the attested copies (catch me parting with the originals!) with that old fellow down in the Masonic Temple. You know him. Your guardian, I mean," to Alice. "I seemed to knock him off his perch. He's in a great stew. He told me you were to be married Wednesday, 1 think, so I made tracks as fast as I could to have a look at my little cousin, and let her know I've a sense of justice, and, though I'll have my rights, I'm not going to be hard on a young lady, and a pretty one into the bargain."

An awful fear shot through Nevin's soul. Was this a claimant for Alice's inheritance?

"If you are a cousin," she exclaimed, "I shall be very glad, for I don't seem to have any one belonging to me, and you are a little like a picture of my father's brother John that hangs in the parlor at home."

"Good! shake on it. *You* look like an honest girl. I suspect you're in luck," turning to Nevin, after shaking Alice's hand vigorously.

"May I ask to what rights you allude?" asked the former, with cold gravity.

"Great Scott! The right to all my father's property and cash of course," returned the stranger, promptly. I intend, in justice to myself, to prove who I am and to what I am entitled; but I won't be greedy if you are friendly. Now, as I feel strange, not to say lost, in this big city, and you seem to have a roomy house, I suppose I may as well take up my quarters with you."

Alice looked white and frightened. Nevin was too confused to reply, so his young fiancée explained :

"This is not my house or Mr. Nevin's. His sister, Mrs. Craven, rents it, but I believe the lease expires in a few days."

"Ha! that alters the case. Well, a man on the cars from 'Frisco told me to put up at the Sherman. I only arrived late last night, so I'll just stay on there. You see, I have been away in New Zealand digging for gold, kauri gum and everything else. I thought I would take a trip this year to see the great World's Fair and the old man, who had not seen me for over twenty-five years. When I arrived in 'Frisco I tumbled across an old friend of my father's, who told me of his death and the property he had left and how it had all been seized by my cousin—naturally enough. I got some lawyers to hunt things up, found you were in Chicago, and here I am. I don't think you are too glad to see me."

"You must admit your appearance on the scene is a little startling," said Nevin. "Have you seen Mr, Bond, the more active of the two guardians?"

"Not yet. The other old boy talked of him and seemed too frightened to say yes or no without him."

"Suppose we go and call on Bond together," said Nevin, pleasantly. "I don't want to make myself ridiculous by over-suspicion, but I am sure you are too much a man of the world to expect that I should take you simply on your own word."

"Right you are," cried the stranger, starting up. "Come along, then; I'll see you again, my pale little cousin." Another strong grasp of the hand and he strode out of the room as abruptly as he had come in.

Nevin paused a moment to say: "This threatens to be a serious affair, Alice. You had better keep out of that Kanaka's way. I'll tell Jeams to send Mary to you as soon as she comes in; let her know everything," and he went hurriedly out of the room.

Alice had a very vague idea of what it all meant.

If this stranger was really a cousin she would be glad. His face was kindly in spite of his fierce eyes, and he might be a friend. Her clearest impression was that Mr. Nevin was very gravely and certainly not pleasurably affected by his sudden appearance. Why should he be? What were the rights he talked about, and what had she to do with them? Until Mrs. Craven came in it was useless to conjecture.

So Alice turned to leave the room and calm herself in her own. As she did so her eyes fell on the wedding-ring which Nevin had been in the act of trying on when her self-called cousin broke in upon them.

It had been thrown aside, paper and all, on a small tea-table, utterly forgotten by the donor. Alice took it up with a sort of prophetic doubt. "How will the coming of this strange man affect our life?" She only thought that if this Ashland, as he called himself, proved really to be a relative, it might worry Nevin to associate with him.

At last, reaching the shelter of her own room, she took refuge from her confused thoughts in a book Harold Neale had once recommended. She was interrupted after more

than an hour had elapsed by a tap at her door,
immediately followed by the entrance of Mrs.
Craven in her outdoor dress.

"They say you want to speak to me, Alice."

"Yes; I want to speak to you very much,"
and she drew forward an easy-chair. "I—we
rather, Mr. Nevin and myself—had a visit from
a wild-looking man who says he is my cousin,"
and she described the interview very accurately.

As Mrs. Craven listened she grew graver and
graver, her mouth closing tightly. When Alice
ceased to speak she said, almost in Nevin's
words:

"This is very serious. If this man turns out
to be what he represents himself, it will change
your fortunes considerably."

"Why will it change my fortunes?" asked
Alice.

"Tell me," said Mrs. Craven, not heeding
her, "did you ever hear of your uncle having a
son?"

"I never did."

"You see, if this man *is* your cousin and the
son of your father's brother, he is entitled to
all his father's property. But it is most likely
a bold attempt to extort money. He will probably offer to compromise matters, but we will
look narrowly into his pretensions. So do not
worry yourself, dear, until you know more."

"No, I shall not. I always had enough, you know, and there's the house at Santa Cruz. I suppose he cannot take that—it was my father's."

Mrs. Craven looked at her with an expression half wondering, half contemptuous.

"You are right not to meet trouble half-way. I can only hope this man will prove an impostor. If not—" She stopped abruptly. "It won't do to think about it. Wilfred has gone with him to Mr. Bond's, has he? I shall not go out till he returns. What shall you do?"

"I will stay with you; I have no objection to meet people," said Alice. "Why are you so frightened about me? Surely you disturb yourself too much."

"Perhaps so. Well, change your dress and join me in the drawing-room."

Mrs. Craven left her abruptly, thinking as she went: "Dress, indeed! If this cannibal proves his story, who is to pay for the lovely trousseau I have chosen? It will half ruin poor Alice. What an idiot she is! Yet I rather like her. How awkward it will be for Wilfred if he is obliged to break with her! No doubt I'll have to attend to that. Men always expect their sisters, their mothers or their wives to do their dirty work."

Mrs. Craven was not less amiable to her vis-

itors that afternoon for the unpleasant anticipations weighing on her mind.

Alice, who since her engagement was announced had grown more assured and self-
possessed, feeling she had a certain right to her
position in the household, talked a little and
listened a good deal to two Michigan Avenue
dames, who pronounced her a nice, sensible
girl.

Mrs. Craven observed her with surprise and
some compassion. How little she realized the
rocks ahead ! Her eyes often sought the clock.
When would these tiresome people go ? when
would Wilfred return ?

That gentleman, meanwhile, lost no time in
getting to the city with the strange claimant.
They scarcely spoke, though Ashland occasionally exclaimed at the crowd, the magnificent
buildings, the crowds of people waiting to cross
here and there.

Arrived at the Masonic Temple, they found
Bond closeted with Mr. Watts, and were
obliged to wait a few minutes in the outer
office. When they were shown into Mr. Bond's
room they found that worthy in an evident
state of perturbation ; he was examining some
papers which lay on the table.

Bond jumped up and seized Nevin's hand, exclaiming :

"A most extraordinary event, a most unfortunate business! A—this—a—is the gentleman in question, I presume?" turning his eyes
with an expression of dislike and dread at the
tall, audacious-looking stranger who towered
above him.

"Yes," said Nevin; "I thought it as well to
come on here at once, and get to the bottom of
the affair."

"And I think it as well to give you this address," said Ashland, taking a piece of paper
from his pocket. "'Mr. S. Lloyd, Agent,
Bank of New Zealand, Montgomery Street,
San Francisco, Cal.' There you are. And
you may as well take my lawyer's card," and
he handed them another: "'C. E. Webb, At-
torney-at-law, Kearny Street, San Francisco,
Cal.' You'll find you can't dispute my iden-
tity. Webb knew my father and myself before I went on the *Jeremiah Thompson* to
New Zealand; so make haste and get through
all the necessary formalities," and turning to
Nevin: "If you show me a proper spirit, you
and my cousin will find I am no niggard.
There a. · my papers; you just look them
through, and you'll see they are all right." And
with this last remark he turned and left the room.

"Do you believe this fellow's story?" asked
Nevin, throwing himself into a chair.

"I'm sure I do not know what to think," said Mr. Watts, dejectedly.

"And I'm sure I don't know what to do," cried Bond, nibbling the top of his pen with a look of vicious irritation. "I knew John Ashland had a son, but he concluded he was dead and gone years and years ago; in fact, I believe he heard so, and that's why he left no will and Alice succeeded to the property as next of kin."

"And what do these papers show?" asked Nevin.

"These are the duly attested copies of his father's marriage certificate, the register of his own birth, the discharge from the ship *Jeremiah Thompson* and a letter from a New Zealand banker stating that he knew the bearer, Thomas Ashland, since his arrival in New Zealand. Yes, yes, it's all right as he says, and here he is—an ugly customer, I can tell you, especially if the man he mentioned, Webb, knows him ; Webb is O. K."

"We must look well to the authenticity of these certificates. What do you intend to do?" asked Nevin.

"Send out an agent to New Zealand," began Mr. Watts.

"Ay ! and who is to pay for it ? " interrupted Bond, with a sneer. "If this man proves his claim Alice Ashland has only her father's pittance."

"It looks bad for my poor little ward," said Mr. Watts, with much feeling. "I think you had better submit the case for counsel's opinion."

"There's nothing to give an opinion about," cried Bond, with a vicious snap. "If this Ashland's story is true, why, he takes everything."

"Well, I shall write to San Francisco immediately," said Mr. Watts. "For the present I will bid you good-day. I am a good deal upset—a—I shall see you early to-morrow."

Nevin stood up while he left the room, and then drawing his seat close to Bond's desk, looked full at the latter, saying, in a low tone:

"Our bargain is at an end, I suspect. I am in a devil of a fix."

"I daresay you are; but what's your case to mine? My hard earnings, the little profits I counted on, torn out of my grasp, and Webb, and this—this unscrupulous Maori, or whatever they call them, routing out all the accounts I have kept so—so carefully, picking holes with what I did for the best and misinterpreting my honest intentions."

"Yes, I suspect he'll skin you," said Nevin, cruelly. "Look here, do you think we shall be obliged to admit his claim?"

"Looks like it."

"And my wedding is fixed for the day after to-morrow. Shade of Cæsar! I am at my wits' end. If I break with Alice and this man turns out an impostor, I shall be sold, indeed. If I marry her and he succeeds, I shall be ruined and undone. Come what may, the wedding must be put off."

"I don't care a fig what you do," cried Bond, with a ghastly grin. "Your elegant sister may help the lame dog over the ditch. I have enough to do with my own affairs. It was an evil hour for me when I first saw you."

"I wish you good-day, Mr. Bond," cried Nevin, in a fury, and, seizing his hat, he abruptly left the room.

CHAPTER X.

NEVIN and his sister held high counsel that night when they were alone.

"You *must* hold on, Wilfred, for a little while. Suppose this Ashland, as he calls himself, turns out to be an impostor, how furious you would be with your own cowardice."

"But what is to be done? I am on the brink of a precipice."

"What a stupid man you are, Wilfred! You must put off the marriage."

"What possible excuse can I urge?"

"There is one before your eyes. The settlements just ready for signature are nullified, or would be if this man's claims hold good. Of course, if we were certain her claim to the property could not be shaken, it would be a good opportunity of doing the passionate and dispensing with settlements altogether," she laughed. "As it is, you must allow yourself to be persuaded by *me*, for Alice's sake, to give up the immediate ceremony. She will never suspect anything. Then, if hers is the losing side, you can back out. I am quite sorry for Alice—she will be adrift again."

"She will not break her heart, that you may rely on. Personally, I shall not be sorry to be clear of the whole affair. I am bored to death. I wish you or the major would give me a thousand dollars."

"I think I will broach the subject to her to-night," said Mrs. Craven, who had not listened to him. "I have already stopped all preparations for the wedding. What do you say, Wilfred—shall I speak to Alice to-night?"

"Yes, by all means. In fact, I am dying for sleep, and will go and forget my troubles for a few hours. I leave myself in your hands, Mary.

I'm afraid the game's played out. Be sure you see the major's lawyers in the morning."

Alice had only felt vaguely disturbed. She saw that Nevin was greatly preoccupied. It was a little remarkable that he made no attempt to speak with her alone, no effort to impart his uneasiness or to ascertain if *she*, too, were depressed.

It was rather a relief to Alice when Mrs. Craven sent for her next morning and opened the subject of the wedding.

"Poor Wilfred is half crazy, dear," she said, as she drew Alice to sit beside her on a sofa in her dressing-room. "I begged him to let me tell you I have insisted on your marriage being postponed for two or three weeks, as much on your account as anything else. You see, if this dreadful New Zealander turns out to be really your cousin, the deed of settlement which was prepared would be useless, and your interests must be cared for."

"Thank you," said Alice, "but I do not understand having any interest separate from— from Mr. Nevin's."

"Very nice and sweet of you to say so, but sentiment is quite out of place in matters of business. Another thing, dear—if it turns out that this cousin of yours can rob you of your fortune, poor Wilfred must get some appoint-

ment before he can have a home to offer
you."

Mrs. Craven watched her narrowly as she
spoke.

"Why not?" asked Alice, quietly. "I am
very young and ignorant. I should, perhaps,
make a better wife later on."

"She is utterly indifferent to him," thought
Mrs. Craven, "and it will be harder to en-
lighten indifference than love." But she said
aloud: "It is a comfort to speak to so sensible
a girl. Now there is no use being miserable.
Put on your cream surah and lace dress and
Major Craven shall drive you over to the Fair
grounds. You are quite a favorite with him
and he hasn't a thing to do, while I have no
end of bothers; really, I don't know why I
trouble so much about other people," concluded
Mrs. Craven, with the air of a martyr and a
sigh of relief at the prospect of being from
Alice's presence for a whole day.

A very unpleasant interval succeeded this
sudden reversal of all their plans.

Nevin absented himself a good deal, and when
he joined his sister and Alice, was so moody
and preoccupied that the latter was half frightened at the complete change in her hitherto
observant and debonair lover.

During this period Ashland called more than

once, but was refused admittance; the bland butler reported to Mrs. Craven that "he threatened to lift me out of the road next time if I didn't let him in." In the butler's opinion the gentleman was a dangerous lunatic.

Finally, Messrs. Bland & Twist, the learned and respectable lawyers of Major Craven, advised their client and his brother-in-law that Mr. Thomas Ashland's claim was not to be disputed, and that the sooner matters were settled in a friendly spirit the better for Miss Ashland's interests.

"I'll go to her directly she comes in and just tell her our engagement must be at an end," said Nevin, on receipt of this intelligence. "It's all a mockery hanging on in this way. Where is Alice gone?" he concluded.

"To meet her cousin at Mr. Watts's rooms, and have everything explained to her. I wonder how much she will understand of it?"

"More than you think. I fancy she will be as sharp as any of you when she is four-and-twenty. All she wants is cultivation. She will always have the advantage of a slow circulation."

"Why, Wilfred, you really seem to dislike the poor child!"

"No; but I resent the loss of time and the immense amount of trouble she has cost me."

"I am sure *your* time is not of much value."

"I wish you'd lend me a hundred dollars. I'm sure Galindo will win at Hawthorne track to-day."

"Wilfred, you are an idiot!"

Mrs. Craven went on with her writing, while her brother talked at intervals without receiving much attention.

Seeing this, Nevin seized a book and settled himself in an easy-chair. He had not read long when he was interrupted by the entrance of Alice, followed, to his surprise, by Ashland, who was got up quite picturesquely.

Alice looked very grave, but in no way disturbed. "Well, dear, I hope you have got through this unpleasant business satisfactorily," said Mrs. Craven, determined to make things as pleasant as she could. "Mr. Ashland, I presume?"

"Yes, I'm Tom Ashland, and as I said before, now that I have my rights I'll show you I am a corker; I'll be a real kinsman to my cousin, though I have robbed her of the inheritance you thought she had."

"The robbing has been on my side, I am afraid," said Alice. "Mr. Bond has been explaining to me that the money I have been spending so freely of late is really my cousin's and ought to be refunded."

"I don't want it," said Ashland, abruptly and firmly; "if I did, that snuffy old liar ought to pay me out of the savings of your long minority. I haven't done with him yet. My lawyer, Webb, has had an interview with his sister and got at more than her precious brother thinks. You and she never spent more than eight hundred or nine hundred dollars a year, you couldn't from what she told Webb. Now, what has Bond done with the difference? I'm sure he'd take a penny from a blind man's hat."

"Your cousin is quite graphic," said Mrs. Craven to Alice, with a pleasant laugh.

"Bond is an unprincipled old scoundrel!" cried Nevin, heartily.

"Yes, my cousin Alice has been robbed right and left. I shall be glad to see her safe under the protection of a good honest fellow," and he nodded to Nevin. "Now, I'll tell you what it is. Come to the Sherman to-morrow between ten and twelve, Mr. Nevin; we'll talk over the new marriage settlements, and you'll see I am prepared to do the thing handsomely."

He smiled a patronizing but good-natured smile. Then, drawing himself to his full height, he added: "I've led a queer life—a life that would make *you* open your eyes" (to Nevin), "much as you know; but it hasn't made a heartless blackguard of me. Now I'll go; I don't want to trouble you with more of my company than is needful. I am not your sort," turning to Mrs. Craven, "nor you mine. Once my cousin is out of your house, I'll never enter it again. But I have a right to look after her, and *I'll do it;* so good-morning." He shook hands with Alice; then, grasping Nevin's with startling energy, "To-morrow before eleven, then," he said; "we'll soon put things straight," and he stalked out of the room.

Mrs. Craven rang the bell, exclaiming: "Quite an effective exit, I declare;" then catching an expressive glance from her brother, she continued: "Now I shall leave you; I daresay you have plenty to talk about."

"Plenty to talk about!" repeated Nevin, as soon as the door closed upon her. "No, rather one painful topic that I dread and evade." He spoke gravely, yet with a certain coldness in his tone, and paused.

"Do not fear to speak to me on any topic," returned Alice, looking kindly and candidly at him.

"Mine is an ungracious task," resumed Nevin, beginning again to pace the room; "but I must not shrink from it. I feel it only just toward you to set you free from any engagement to myself. I will not drag you down

to poverty for my own selfish gratification.
No, Alice, I release you, and trust you will
have a fairer lot than to share the banishment
that must be my destiny."

Alice was greatly amazed, and even affected.
She was so profoundly convinced of his deep and
warm attachment to herself that she never
hesitated to offer with simple kindness to
share his destiny, however dark or repul-
sive.

"I am not easily frightened," she said, with
a sweet smile and downcast eyes that might
well have charmed a true lover. " I should not
be worthy to be your wife if I shrank from
sharing the rough as well as the smooth places
in your road. I have not been accustomed to
luxury or finery, and I may yet be as really
necessary as you used to say I was."

"Jupiter!" thought Nevin to himself, "she
is not going to let me off. I was right; she is
sharper than Mary imagined.—My dear girl,"
he said aloud, in a more natural manner, "you
really don't know what you are talking about.
Life is very costly, even to a miserable bachelor;
but when it comes to married life, it is a crime
to marry with insufficient means. So long as
there was enough, I was far too much in love
to care on which side the money was. Now all
is changed. No, dear Alice, marriage is out of

the question. Let us conquer all selfish weakness and part."

His voice, even more than his words, enlightened Alice. A sudden consciousness that he wanted to get rid of the engagement dawned upon her with vivid, mortifying clearness.

"Very well," she said, in a low tone, raising her eyes steadily to his, "if I am not necessary to your happiness the engagement had much better come to an end. But why did you tell me what was not true? Can a fortnight have destroyed what you told me was so deeply rooted in your heart?"

"My dear Alice," cried Nevin, blithely, "you should make allowance for my feeling that I was by no means essential to you. Come now, be candid and let us part friends. You are not the least in love with me?"

"I do not know much about love, Mr. Nevin; but when you assured me that you loved me and could not face your life without me I was greatly surprised, but I believed you. I was very grateful. Now it is very unpleasant, but we can part without much suffering. So goodby. I will send you all your many presents through Mrs. Craven. The *last*," with slight emphasis, "is, I believe, in the silver casket in the drawing-room."

Her simplicity and composure had a curious effect on Nevin. He felt as he could fancy a man might do after being kicked—cowed and degraded.

"Believe me, I shall ever retain the warmest regard, the highest esteem," began Nevin, holding out his hand.

Alice looked at him with a smile, a quiet smile, gave him her hand for a moment and left him.

"That is well ended," he said to himself, "but she knows how to strike home. I must get hold of Mary."

Alice' reached her room with her cheeks flushed and her hands trembling. It is true she was not in love with Nevin, but the notion of a settled home soothed and satisfied her. Now everything was wrenched away ; she was despised, rejected, friendless. Gradually, however, her quiet good sense came to her aid ; she had really done nothing to be ashamed of. Was she to blush because, being herself true, she believed Nevin to be the same? No, she would not allow herself to be overwhelmed. Her first effort must be to escape from Mrs. Craven's ; so she sat quietly down and wrote to Mr. Watts and Mr. Bond, telling them that the marriage was broken off, and that she would like to leave for California immediately, and implored Mr. Bond to let his sister join her there.

Then she felt calm and equal to meeting Mrs. Craven.

These were dreadful days of trial to Mr. Watts. He never knew when he was safe from the incursions of the reckless New Zealander, no longer able to pass on all his responsibilities to his colleague, Mr. Bond, nor to escape the searching queries of the new heir, who fulminated the most tremendous accusations against the acting guardian and almost called him rascal to his face.

The day after Nevin had succeeded in shaking off the shackles of his engagement Tom Ashland descended on the victimized Mr. Watts, before he had quite swallowed his breakfast.

"This is a pretty how-do-you-do," he ejaculated, throwing a letter on the table and drawing a chair violently opposite to Mr. Watts. "That hound Nevin has broken with Miss Ashland. There, read that! I appointed him to be with me this morning to talk over a new settlement and intended to make a handsome addition to my cousin's little fortune. I understood he agreed to come, and instead I get this precious document."

Mr. Watts, with an air of resignation, took it up and read the contents. It stated in cold, clear terms that Miss Ashland and himself had agreed to break off the engagement and consequently there could be no use in Nevin keeping the appointment with him.

"Well, what do you think of that?"

"Ahem! I am not much surprised on the whole," said Mr. Watts, slowly. "You see, it was entirely a marriage of convenience on his part."

"Then why did you consent to it?" asked Ashland, angrily.

"Well, you see, it was hard to know what to do with the young lady, and Mr. Bond thought—"

"Never mind what *he* thought! He'd sell her to the blackest imp in hell for a dime. I suspect, for all he is such a fine gentleman, Nevin and your right-bower understood each other."

"Not that I know of, I assure you, Mr. Ashland. He—" But Watts was not destined to finish his sentence. Another letter was laid before him, which in his turn he handed to Ashland. It was Alice's expressive little note.

"Ha! it is a regular split, then," cried Ashland. "I suppose nothing is to be done?"

"Well, no; a breach of promise of marriage case is not to be thought of."

"No—by heavens! no. I was hesitating

whether I should lick the scoundrel or not. I'd
like to kick him from Auckland to Timam. Yes,
we must get her out of that house at once. Just
you step down to that sky-scraper and tell old
Bond to wire his sister to meet Alice and me in
'Frisco. We can stay at Monterey until those
tenants of his get out of her own house. I'll
wire Webb to secure suitable rooms for Alice,
Mrs. Williams and myself. Shall I go and see
Alice? No, I'd better not; I'd spoil that
masher's mug if I saw him. Give me pen, ink
and paper; I'll drop her a line and tell her
to keep her heart up, and another to Nevin,
telling him he is a good riddance. Where's
your blotter?

"There," he said, as he finished his two
short notes; "that will settle Nevin, and I
hope my little kinswoman will feel she is not
without a backer when she reads this. Mind
you write, too, as kind as you can. And don't
forget to tell Bond, if he doesnt't let his sister
join Alice I'll put him in Joliet. In whatever
I may be obliged to undertake against him
I can, of course, count on your help, Mr.
Watts, otherwise you are an accomplice; and
I believe you are an honest, well-meaning man.
Good-by to you!" He clattered away noisily,
leaving Mr. Watts in a state of collapse.

After a while he pulled himself together, and

went away in much agitation to see Bond, whom he found in an indescribable condition of rage, despair and terror, his necktie twisted around under his left ear, his spectacles pushed up above his eyebrows.

"Oh, Mr. Watts, it's you, is it? I little thought you'd be talked over by that madman to turn against your best friend, for that I have been to you, helping you every way I could, even to my own loss (there's half a year's interest due on the little loan I got you last fall); and what right has he got to come here worrying over the savings of his cousin's minority? He'll turn against *you* next. His friend, Mr. Webb, was here yesterday, and says his mother was as mad as a hatter. What will he be after next? He can't even leave that stupid creature of a sister of mine alone. It's the devil's own bad luck that sent him here to upset everything. Look here, now, I'll have nothing more to say to you and your ward; and how will you get on by yourself, I'd like to know?"

"You have been of very great service to me, I acknowledge, Mr. Bond; but the affairs of the minor are not so complicated as to be beyond my power to—to conduct. I must say, I think you made a great mistake when you—"

"Lord, what a weather-cock you are!" in-

terrupted the other, with a contemptuous toss
of his chin. "Was it my fault that this New
Zealander has turned up to set Lake Michigan
on fire?"

After much recrimination and squabbling it
was agreed on between the spider and the fly
that everything must present a smooth surface
to the new actor who had appeared so inopportunely to interfere with Bond's little game,
even if it cost money to repair a few of the well-meaning mistakes which unavoidably occurred
from overzeal in the minor's service.

Thomas Ashland's energy was of the feverish order. He sent his lawyer, Webb, via the
Union Pacific to San Francisco, to secure rooms
at some quiet retreat near Monterey or Santa
Cruz for himself, Alice and Mrs. Williams,
whom Webb was to call on en route; then he
forced Bond to telegraph his sister, authorizing her to meet Mr. and Miss Ashland and return to the latter's employment.

To Alice the hours which intervened between
her parting with Nevin and the moment of her
leaving Mrs. Craven's were painful in an irritaing sense. The consciousness of having been
so completely deceived lowered her in her own
estimation, and though far from perceiving how
completely Mrs. Craven had been her brother's

accomplice, common sense suggested that she could not be completely innocent of his schemes. Indeed, this interval was nearly as distressing and irritating to Mrs. Craven as to her guest. Even Mrs. Craven's world-hardened self-possession was ruffled by the constant presence of the guileless young creature she had assisted to blind.

The only allusion Alice made to the sudden rupture of her engagement was when she gave Mrs. Craven the packet containing Nevin's gifts, saying : " This is for your brother. You know what it is. Do not let us say anything more about him. I have a note from Mr. Watts ; he promises to take me away to-morrow, or next day at furthest, so I need hamper your movements no longer. You have been very, very good to me, whether you really like me or not, and I am heartily grateful."

" My dear," cried Mrs. Craven, with tears in her beautiful eyes (they came quite readily whenever she wanted them), " no words can express how grieved and ashamed I feel. It is all too painfully fresh to talk about now. Later I hope to explain away some of the blame which naturally seems to attach to me." So saying, she kissed her brow, patted her shoulder and hurried away to give orders respecting the packing up.

Thomas Ashland was announced the next morning, and Alice felt like a prisoner about to be released.

"Now, are you ready to start? We must catch the one-o'clock for 'Frisco. I suppose you can come at once?"

"Yes, I can; but I'm ashamed to say I have too much baggage for a coupe."

"Well, we'll get an express, then. Now, go get on your things and say good-by if it's necessary. I don't want to see Mrs. Double-face again."

"Mrs. Craven is out. I hardly like to leave without seeing her."

"Nonsense!" growled Ashland, in his hardest tones. "If they had her in Timam she'd be picking oakum. I shall not leave you in this house any longer, so hurry up."

Alice was somewhat afraid of Ashland—his height, deep voice and rugged manners made her shrink into herself. Moreover, she knew that any one looking at the bare facts of the case would not think her charming hostess deserving of much consideration, though she could not help liking her. She compromised matters, however, by writing a few lines of farewell, which she left in the hands of her maid, and hastily donned her traveling attire.

As soon as Alice left the room Ashland applied himself vigorously to the bell, which immediately evoked the splendid apparition of the butler.

"I say, get down Miss Ashland's trunks, and call an express; look alive, will you, and there's for your trouble."

The tip was handsome enough to make him, in Chicago parlance, "get a move on himself," and he responded with a gracious "Thank'ee sir," and retired to execute the "tipper's" commands.

It was with a new sense of safety and exhilaration that Alice found herself being whirled along over the Union Pacific to San Francisco, where she and her cousin arrived safe and sound on the fourth day, to find her old companion, Mrs. Williams, awaiting her at the Lick House. To be sitting opposite to Mrs. Williams in the old familiar fashion, as if the last two months had been an unsubstantial dream, was something so strange and delightful that she could hardly persuade herself that her ardent desire was really fulfilled. She was tempted every now and then to catch her arm or seize her hand, to assure herself it was really her old friend in the flesh.

By degrees she mastered her excitement and they fell into their old confidential tone. Alice, before she slept the first night in California, had told the whole story of her engagement and its mortifying conclusion. Over this recital she shed no tears, and the mental exercise seemed to clear her own impressions and reveal to her the systematic deception practiced on her in its fullness. The strongest feeling left in her mind was a conviction that there was something in herself not lovable, as the man she liked had avoided her because she showed her liking, and the man who seemed to like her forsook her with unflattering readiness directly she proved deficient in those solid attractions which real and personal estates possess.

"Ah, dear Williams," said Alice, at the end of her story, "if you had not deserted me I might have escaped a good deal. I should not have made so great a fool of myself."

"Ah, dear, but I couldn't help it," cried Mrs. Williams, eagerly. "I won't submit to seem a cold-hearted, selfish creature. I did not desert you of my own free will, that you may be sure. I never said a word against my brother before, but I am mad at him, and you are wiser and older and won't betray me. I have had to obey him. He has been hard on me. You know I am a widow, with one boy, kind and gentle, but weak and easily led, and God only knows what I went through to give him food and clothes and a little schooling. At last I was struck down with illness, and then I was obliged to beg my brother for bread. He wasn't bad, for he gave me a trifle and sent me to look after you. My dear child, it healed my heart to have you to love. Well, my brother took Johnny into his office and promised to look after him, but he was just an unpaid errand-boy. One unlucky day my poor boy, who had fallen in with bad companions, was tempted to try his luck at Garfield Park races, and won and won, and then lost all. Robert had, for a wonder, left some gold and notes just inside his desk and my misguided boy took some of it, thinking he would win back everything; but he lost. Oh! it was an awful time. Well, to end the story, Johnny was sent away to Cleveland, Ohio, to learn the building trade, and when Bob wrote for me to leave the cottage at Santa Cruz I refused; but he sent word that if I didn't do as he bade me he would expose Johnny and warn his employers that he was a thief. What was I to do?"

Here Mrs. Williams broke down and sobbed loudly. Alice kneeled down by her and soothed her with tender caresses, exclaiming with indignant fervor against Bond's unfeeling harshness.

"But why did he want to separate us?" asked Alice, with a puzzled look.

"Your cousin swears that Bob sold you to Mrs. Craven and her brother, but was sold himself, because he, Mr. Ashland, turned up. He is a kind, generous man, that Mr. Ashland."

"Yes, he is; he is indeed; but I am afraid of him. I don't know why, but I am certainly afraid of him."

"Nonsense, my dear; he will be a good, kind friend, and he will not stand any of Bob's tricks."

"Well, thank Heaven, we are together again," said Alice. "I want no more finery, or grand people, only to be at rest and safe." Then the tears stole from under her downcast lids, and she had the relief that a copious though quiet flood of tears affords.

Thomas Ashland found himself pretty busy in San Francisco, and Alice was rather astonished at his many absences from her. One evening, however, about a week after their arrival, he dined with them at the hotel, and proposed a trip to the Golden Gate Park. "It is a lovely evening," said Ashland, "and one can hardly breathe here. Get your hat and sketchbook and we'll drive through the park to the Cliff House. There will be some air to be had on the beach. I'd like to see you sketch the 'seal-rocks' on the spot. It seems a wonderful thing to be able to do it."

"Very well," said Alice, readily enough. She was always glad to shake off thought and memory by motion, and missed, more than she would like to say, her frequent drives with Mrs. Craven.

"Ah! the air is fresher out here," said Ashland, as they approached the cliff; "it may bring some color to your cheeks. I don't like to see you so white."

"It's my nature, Thomas."

"When we get to Monterey you'll be all right. I fancy you'd like life in New Zealand. Most wonderful country on earth." And he talked on not badly, describing his adventures among the Maoris, his ascent of Mount Cook, the wonderful Rotamahana lakes, the marvelous pink and white terraces of Tarewera, etc.

Alice listened with interest and sympathy, asking a leading question here and there, and so, in good humor with each other, they reached a spot on the beach where Alice thought she might attempt a sketch of the world-famed "seal-rocks." Alice was not easily satisfied with her work and rubbed out a good deal. At last she succeeded in making a very fair sketch of the scene before her, which elicited strong expressions of approbation from her cousin.

She began slowly to close and strap her book and pencil-case. Ashland rose, stretched himself and sat down again.

"I say," he exclaimed, "it wasn't very nice for that old Bond, putting down your wedding clothes in his bill of accounts."

"He did not mean anything unpleasant," returned Alice, coloring faintly.

"Perhaps not. But I say, Alice, if you'd rather not have them wasted, or you'd like just to stamp out all memory of that unlucky business, I am quite at your service. Suppose you marry me? Then, you know, you'd get the property back again."

He looked at her earnestly as he spoke, but without the least of a loverlike expression.

Alice almost dropped her book. "What can have put such an idea into your head?" she exclaimed, in profound amazement.

"Well, you see, it's the best sort of way to make matters comfortable for you; so—"

"You are kindly disposed to sacrifice yourself for my comfort. Thank you, Thomas," and she laughed merrily, but not unkindly. "Why, you don't care the least for me."

"Yes, I do. I am very fond of you. I don't mean to say I am in love. I have been in love two or three times, and it was a desperate business. You really might do worse; I'm not a bad-looking fellow. You might keep me in order; we would have plenty of money and grow fond of each other. Now just think it over."

" You are very kind," said Alice, still laughing. " I never thought any one would be so accommodating. Seriously, never let us talk of this project again. I am sure you will agree with me, when you reconsider your kind wish to prevent my trousseau being useless."

" All right," Ashland exclaimed. "I suppose you know what you want; and I daresay you are a great deal too good for me, so we will say no more about it. I'll be your friend, only if you change your mind let me know."

" Oh, yes," said Alice, smiling, " I will propose for you in due form."

Ashland laughed. " I'm your man, if you will," he said. " I've not been as steady as I ought, and I've a notion that a wife and a home would settle me."

No more was said on the subject. Alice was a good deal startled and amazed, but Ashland seemed to forget the conversation completely. He was very irregular in his ways; he would call every now and then, and then absent himself for a week. When he reappeared he generally looked ill and haggard. " I'm always bothered with headaches," he said, when Alice asked if he felt unwell. "I have had one or two bad bouts lately, and as I am not fit to be spoken to I keep out of the way when they come on. I would take you to Monterey at once, but Webb cannot find a house for rent, and I hate these big hotels; I'm not used to them."

"A great friend of mine," said Mrs. Williams, "used to keep a very superior boarding-house about four miles out of Monterey, a beautiful house with a conservatory. It's years since I heard of her. I'll give you her address, Mr. Ashland; you might inquire about her, and if she's still there, I know that you'd enjoy her surroundings. Her terms are high, but there's every comfort."

"Oh, we needn't put on the screw," said Ashland, who, though ready to exact the last cent from Bond, was lavish in providing any luxury or amusement for the kinswoman he had taken under his somewhat tyrannical protection. "Will you get me a glass of brown pop," he continued, "and write the address for me? I shall start early to-morrow. We'll leave here this week."

"Well, you *are* abstemious," cried Mrs. Williams, admiringly, as she handed him the beverage. "Are you a total abstainer?"

"Not quite," returned Ashland; "but this

is better than old rye. Well, I'll report to you
the day after to-morrow ; so good-night. I
will be off early in the morning, and we will
make all arrangements when I come back."

"How very kind he is!" cried Alice, when
he had left. "I wish—"

"What, my dear—what do you wish?"

"I wish I were not so afraid of him sometimes. When he walks up and down and
seems looking at something far away that dis-
pleases him, I do not quite like to be in the
room with him."

"Ah! that's only when his poor head has
been bad. I'm sure he would do anything on
earth for you."

Under Thomas Ashland's energetic guidance
things were soon in train for Alice's change of
abode. He had succeeded in finding Mrs. Williams's old friend. She was still the proud pro-
prietor of a very successful boarding-house,
and was highly pleased at the idea of receiving
Mrs. Williams and her charge. The liberal
arrangements of Mr. Ashland met her entire
approval, and a few days later Alice and her
chaperon settled in Mrs. Jarrett's comfortable
mansion—Mission House.

The hack which conveyed them to the Southern Pacific Depot had just driven away when
a gentleman, broad-shouldered and dark-eyed,

stepped into the Lick House and inquired of the clerk if Miss Ashland was there.

" They have just driven to the Southern Pacific Depot," said the clerk.

" Do you know where they are going ? "

"I am sure I do not, sir, though I fancy I heard the gentleman mention Monterey."

" The gentleman ! What gentleman ? "

" Mr. Ashland, sir."

" Well, I'll leave my card, at any rate ; they may return to this hotel."

The card was inscribed " Harold Neale." Time had gone heavily with him since his last brief visit to Chicago. He had been more severely hit than he at first thought, and the feeling of profound compassion for Alice, as the victim of Nevin's unprincipled schemes, helped to keep his tenderness for her constantly alive.

He waited and waited for the announcement of the wedding, but none came. He did not like to write to Mrs. Craven for an explanation. So he waited and dreamed, though apparently occupied with the work of harvesting at Peekskill.

Early in August Mrs. Craven came to illuminate Peekskill with her bright presence. On her arrival she sent a message to Harold and trusted to the old attraction to draw him to her side.

Nor was she mistaken. The day but one after her arrival being Sunday, Harold went over a little before noon, looking, Mrs. Craven fancied, darker and graver than ever.

He was welcomed with quiet warmth perceptible to himself only.

After a pause he asked :

"What has become of Nevin ? "

"I do not exactly know at this moment," she returned. "He is somewhere in Dakota, I think. But I have a good deal to tell you by and by."

The weather was so tempting that after a little lunch Harold asked Mrs. Craven if she felt equal to a walk up the hills.

Mrs. Craven was delighted, and went away for her hat and parasol.

Neale thought he had seldom seen a fairer woman as they left the house together. Her dress of thin, pale-brown stuff, with red sash and ribbons, her wide-brimmed straw hat turned up on one side, where a couple of creamy roses lay on her rich hair, the softened, happy expression of her eyes, made up a lovely picture.

"I suppose you are dying to know what happened to break off Wilfred's marriage?" she said, when they were well away from the house.

"I might survive a little longer without the knowledge, but I *should* like to know."

"Hasn't Wilfred written to you since—since the bubble burst?"

"Not a line."

"What an idle fellow he is! He promised he would tell you everything, or I should have done so. Well, here is the story," and she described the sudden appearance of Thomas Ashland, the irresistible character of his claim and the consequent breaking off of the engagement with Nevin.

It was lightly and amusingly told, with a tinge of rose-color on Nevin's share in the business.

"Really," exclaimed Harold, "this has been a trying affair. Nevin has gone off to Dakota, you say? What has become of his loving fiancée?"

"I believe she went back to California and Mrs. Williams. But do you know, I don't think she cared a fig for Wilfred; she was rather obtuse in some directions."

"Then she must have imposed on you very successfully, for in the last letter you were so good as to send me you spoke of the extremely demonstrative nature of her affection. In short, it bored you."

"Did I?" said Mrs. Craven. "I suppose something suggested the idea to me at the time; but looks do not prove deep affection."

"Certainly not," returned Harold, carelessly. "The most ardent caresses are no guarantee for fidelity. They are, no doubt, a matter of temperament."

Mrs. Craven colored.

"You are more philosophic than you were when we last walked here together."

"I should think so," said Harold, laughing. "And, if *your* ideas are not greatly changed since those primitive days, I must have bored you infinitely."

"Do you think you did?" asked Mrs. Craven.

"I dare not answer. Do you think you are able to climb as far as the rock? You remember it?"

"Remember it? Yes," she replied, in a tone that said much more than the words.

Harold struck into a track that led up the side of the hill, and conducted her to their old trysting-place.

Harold talked pleasantly and lightly of the past, of the beautiful scenery, of many things, but Mrs. Craven was silent; she had intended that Harold should, during this visit of hers to the old scenes, avow the bitter agony of feeling that she was lost to him. Now she felt in some indescribable way that the mastery of the situation had passed out of her hands.

At last they reached the well-known spot. Mrs. Craven seated herself on a mossy stone and Neale leaned against the stem of a tree. They both looked out over the fair scene before them for a minute or two, and then their eyes met. No need for words to tell what the other was thinking of, and Mrs. Craven exclaimed, impulsively: "Harold, here, where we last parted, I humbly ask your forgiveness for my heartless, cruel conduct. I was so young and thoughtless. I was scarce responsible. How often since have I longed for a nature stronger, truer than my own to lean on, to—to love as I knew not how to love *then*. I am more lonely than you think, dear Harold. Let me hear you say that you can forgive me, and restore me to something like the position I *once* held in your esteem." She held out her hand, which he took and held for a moment, her beautiful lips quivering, her soft eyes suffused with tears.

"Ah, Mary," returned Harold, touched for a moment, "a man might well forgive you much." Then, in his usual tone: "My dear Mrs. Craven, I by no means deserve so ample an *amende*. Do not give a thought to the past if it brings you pain. I am glad to see you surrounded by everything that can make life bright and pleasant."

"Everything!" echoed Mrs. Craven, turning her eyes full on his. "Yes, heaps of toys, but nothing that can really touch the heart. My husband cares more for his horse than for me. I may do what I like, because he never needs my society. He—"

"Come, come!" interrupted Harold, smiling. "No man ever adored a wife as he does. I really must stand up for the major. He may not be a hero of romance, but he is a right good fellow and quite justifies the opinion you must have formed of him at *one* time."

"I had no opinion at all," she murmured. "I married him because I was told to marry."

"We none of us realize our early dreams," said Harold. "But your. lot has fallen in pleasant places compared to the majority. Look at your quondam protegée, Miss Ashland —a mere shuttlecock between her guardian and intended husband, whose bowels of compassion are mere catgut. She is bought and sold, petted, blinded, flattered till the supreme moment when she is found wanting in her chief title to regard and consideration, and then she is at once dropped, disavowed, sent back to obscurity, from which she was dragged to suit the schemes of those who wished to appropriate her money. What would *you* think and feel had you been subjected to such treatment?"

"My dear Mr. Neale, you are really quite excited. Of course, it was all very bad, and I am ashamed of my part in the affair; but it was a great chance for Wilfred. I hoped all would turn out well; but as it didn't, why, you could not expect Wilfred to marry on nothing. It was unpleasant for Alice. I cannot imagine being subjected to such treatment myself, I confess," looking up with a smile intended to be candid and winning; but Harold's gravity did not relax.

"Yet Miss Ashland is a delicate, tender woman like yourself, with less strength, less experience—a simple, innocent child, the soul of truth and honor. Why—"

"Why," interrupted Mrs. Craven, surprised at his tone, "why, Mr. Neale, you seem to be absolutely in love with that very colorless, good little girl."

"I am," he returned, meeting her eyes fully and calmly. "I was interested in her from the first, but could not interfere with Wilfred, who trusted me all through. Now I reproach myself with acting a cowardly and unmanly part, which, if I can repair, I will."

"Would you marry her?" with a gasp.

"Yes, if I am so fortunate as to win her, which is doubtful. I can fancy nothing sweeter, nothing to be more ardently desired than to find her true eyes, her gentle face by the fireside to welcome one back after the troubles of the day. She is the very embodiment of home."

"It is a pretty picture," said Mrs. Craven, coldly. "But I am feeling a slight chill—shall we return? I. see you think I have deserted your little ideal. It would be awkward and senseless to keep up with her under the circumstances. Besides, if I am any judge of indications, I suspect she will find a potent protector in her Maori cousin."

Mrs. Craven rose decidedly, and though Harold was most careful of her during their descent, the walk back seemed infinitely longer, infinitely more fatiguing, than when they were outward bound.

Two days after this episode a telegram from Major Craven obliged his wife to curtail her visit very abruptly.

As soon as he could Neale escorted his mother to California for the winter, and, having Alice's address from Mr. Bond, called, as we have seen, fruitlessly at Miss Ashland's hotel.

"If—if only the cousin is not a formidable rival! I'd like to see him. I'll not give up, though," he muttered, as he walked slowly down Montgomery Street.

CHAPTER XI.

It was dark and foggy when Mrs. Williams and Alice arrived at Monterey; but the indescribable odor of the soft salt sea breeze of that beautiful spot was very delicious to the latter.

She felt her spirits rise on leaving the bustling and noisy cities far behind her, as if a fresh stream of ideas had been set in motion and the weary languor which had oppressed her been swept away.

Mrs. Williams's old friend, a stout matron with rosy cheeks, a widow's cap and a solid figure, professed herself overjoyed to meet Mrs. Williams again and declared Alice to be a sweet young lady, etc., etc.

Then she ushered them into their apartments.

"And Mr. Ashland was most particular, I assure you. Nothing but the best would do for him. This is a new wing. I built it myself over three years ago. I have had heaps of trouble since last I saw you, Mrs. Williams. But though I have got on wonderful, I couldn't have done that only a poor old gentleman, who

lived four or five years with us and gave such
a lot of trouble that no one had patience with
him but myself, left me some money in his
will. So here is your suite : a sitting-room—
there, you can see the bay out of that window,
and this one opens into the conservatory, and
here are your bedrooms just behind, opening
into each other. I have put a fire in Miss Ashland's room ; she might be a little chilly after
the drive here and the gentleman told me she
wasn't too strong. And now you'll have time
to dress for dinner. I have only a small party
now, but they are quite elegant people."

Having rattled off this long address with
immense volubility, she threw open the bedroom door, stirred up the fire, and with a nod
and a smile bustled away.

"Well, I declare, she is just the same as
ever !" cried Mrs. Williams, beginning to untie
her bonnet strings, " as busy and active, only
a trifle stouter."

"It is quite a pretty room," said Alice, looking around ; "and how much better furnished
than our Chicago lodgings !" Her residence
with Mrs. Craven had developed a taste for
beautiful surroundings which had been rather
a source of suffering lately.

"Oh, I'm sure you'll be delighted when you
get up to-morrow, dear," said Mrs. Williams.
" Now, hadn't you better get ready ? "

The party assembled there was rather small.
Three or four old gentlemen, accustomed to a
yearly trip from the Golden Gate to Monterey,
a childless married couple, a much-traveled

spinster with strong social and political con-
victions, and a sweet-looking old lady with
silvery hair, soft dark eyes and regular, refined
features. She was dressed in black silk and
black lace, and had an air of distinction.

Yet there was something timid and dependent
about her that touched Alice, who sat beside
her at dinner and showed her sundry little attentions which come so natural to the young
of a better class.

Mrs. Williams sat opposite, next the hostess,
who seemed to have much to say, for Mrs.
Williams looked deeply interested in her conversation. Dinner was nearly over before
Alice's neighbor addressed her, then she said:

"You have only just arrived, I believe?"

"Scarcely an hour ago."

"I have been here nearly a week, and find
the air very strengthening and delightful. You
will find the outlook from this house very
pretty."

"I long for daylight," returned Alice, "for
it seems ages since I went to Chicago. I feel
quite excited at the thought of being near the
sea again."

This avowal seemed to interest the old lady,
and they continued to talk at intervals till
dinner was over and the ladies left the room.

Alice paused a moment till Mrs. Williams
joined her. On reaching the hall they found
the white-haired lady standing at the foot of
the stairs, holding one corner of her shawl
against her mouth.

"I am afraid there is a draft here," said Alice, pausing.

"There is a little. I am waiting for Mrs. Jarrett, who is so good as to help me upstairs every day."

"She has been called away, I think," said Alice, and then added, with shy politeness: "Our room is opposite—will you sit down there till Mrs. Jarrett comes? Pray, do."

"You are very good—if I do not trouble you."

"There is a nice fire—do come in," urged Mrs. Williams, and the invitation was accepted.

A little conversation, not too fluent or ready, ensued, and thus a new acquaintance was formed in the outset of this fresh page in Alice's life.

"Well, Mrs. Neale, I could not tell what had become of you," exclaimed the mistress of the house, coming in a few minutes later. "It is very nice for you to be comfortable here. I do hope you'll excuse my seeming neglect, but I was called away. Will you come into the drawing-room to-night, ladies?"

But Alice and Mrs. Williams preferred remaining in their own apartment, and spent a cheerful evening arranging their belongings.

The next morning was bright and beaming. Alice was up early and called Mrs. Williams to share her delight at the view from the window of their sitting-room.

"How lovely! how delightful!" cried Alice. "Oh, let us make haste and get out; 1 long to be down by the sea; you will come with me, will you not?"

"To be sure I will; but I must eat my breakfast first."

"Well, do not be long, dear."

The complete change—the newest of everything—was of infinite benefit to Alice. Yet the lesson she had received taught her the deepest self-distrust. She shrank from making any acquaintance, and was quite happy with her good friend Mrs. Williams and Mrs. Neale, between whom and herself a degree of intimacy sprung up.

Mrs. Neale required much care—care beyond what her hostess could give. She loved reading, but her eyes soon grew weary.

Alice was heartily glad to read to the gentle, cultivated woman by the hour, and enjoyed the discussions which naturally arose on the subjects of their reading. On sunny days the invalid crept to the beach, supported by Alice's arm, and thus soothed and cheered, grew wonderfully better.

Meantime, Alice was not without conjectures as to the possible relationship which might exist between her new friend and the offending Harold. These had been answered at an early stage of their acquaintance by some reference on the part of Mrs. Neale to her home on the far-off Hudson; but even then Alice could not bring herself to mention that she had ever known her son; she had no wish to renew her acquaintance with him.

But now and then there were tones in his

mother's voice, a peculiar, grave, almost sad
smile, that brought Harold Neale back to her
memory with a strange pang amazing to herself.

Of Ashland they saw and heard nothing for
fully a week after they had settled at Mission
House. This was the most extraordinary, as he
had engaged a bedroom to be kept ready for
his occupation ; and Mrs. Jarrett, as well as her
guests, were quite excited about his coming, as
the former had proclaimed him a millionaire of
unbounded generosity and "as handsome a
fellow as ever you saw in your life."

He came, however, one warm, thunderous
afternoon. Alice was struck by his gaunt and
ghastly looks, the dull, sad look of his heavy
eyes.

"Have you been ill, cousin ? " she asked, with
genuine anxiety. " Is that the reason we have
not heard from you or seen you ? "

"Yes. I have had a bad turn this time : an
attack of my old fever and ague, but I'm all
right now. And you are sorry for your un-
couth cousin? I see you are, and that does me
a heap of good. You know I have never had
any one to care for me."

"Well, I do, Tom, and I ought; no one has
been so good to me as you have."

As she spoke a flash of lightning, accompanied by a peal of thunder, made Mrs. Williams cover her face with her hands, exclaiming:
"God bless us ! "

Alice unconsciously clung to Ashland. He
with a sudden gesture threw one arm around

her and pressed her closely to him, almost painfully close. The darkness slightly cleared and Alice, startled, alarmed, quickly disengaged herself.

"I beg your pardon," cried Ashland, confusedly. "I forgot, I believe I was nervous. I didn't know what I was doing. Did I hurt you? You are such a delicate creature I ought never to touch you." He threw himself on the lounge. "When the row is over get me a cup of tea, like a good girl; my head aches still." He pressed his hands to his brow.

Alice hastened to bring the desired beverage herself, placing it with kindliest care on a small table beside the sufferer, and then bathed his brow with eau-de-cologne, all in so simple and sisterly a fashion that the most conceited coxcomb that ever believed in his own irresistible attractions could not have misconstrued her. She gradually recovered the uneasiness his unusual looks and manner had aroused, and by dinner-time all things seemed as usual.

Thomas Ashland's visit lasted three days. He seemed reluctant, yet obliged to go, and made many promises to return soon.

Alice was ashamed of herself : she felt such a relief at his departure. His words had been extremely variable ; often he seemed to struggle against some impulse, some unaccountable ill-temper, of which Alice could not help being conscious. Her attention to Mrs. Neale—why should she give so much of her time to a stranger?

"One might think you were paid to run and

care for that old woman," he growled, just before starting for 'Frisco. "I believe you would rather read to her than talk to me."

"But, cousin, Mrs. Neale is ill and lonely; I am really of some comfort to her. She wants me a great deal more than you do."

"How do you know that? I have more troubles than you know of. Look here, I have a great mind to tell you all about them when I come back; would you care to hear?"

"Yes; I should care very much, indeed," she said, earnestly. "I should be very glad to be of the least use to you."

"Thank you," said Ashland, hoarsely, and he smoked with energy for some moments. "You've a kind heart, Alice, and if loneliness is a claim on it I am lonely enough. Well, when I come back you and I will take a ride together, and I will tell you my troubles. Now, little cousin, good-by; but I'll come back soon— soon." He pressed her hand painfully hard and hurried away, leaving her by no means happy.

CHAPTER XII.

ALL things fell into the ordinary routine when Ashland's disturbing presence was withdrawn, and Alice's readings and conversations with Mrs. Neale grew more frequent and prolonged. She generally spent the evening in her friend's room, as Mrs. Williams deeply enjoyed the gossip and cards in the drawing-room. Although the least inquisitive of mortals, Mrs. Neale asked her young favorite a few questions respecting her relative, which, though very guarded, impressed Alice with the idea that she was somehow distrustful of him.

" I imagine he has known neither mother nor sisters. Family life is of enormous importance to every one, but especially to men ; they need softening so much."

Alice assented ; and as Mrs. Neale did not seem disposed to talk any more, she took up the book they had been reading and began. It was one of Bulwer's novels. Time went quickly ; Alice was absorbed in the trials and tribulations of " Gentleman Waife."

Without, it was a wild night ; within, it was homelike and cheerful. A bright fire and gay chintz hangings, Mrs. Neale in her armchair, Alice in a pretty soft gray dress, with lace about the throat and arms, seated on a low seat, her book on her knees, the lamp on the table beside her, shining down on her graceful head, her earnest, thoughtful face—it was a sweet picture, at least it seemed so to some one who opened the door softly, so softly that for a moment they were not aware a third person was added to their number ; then the sudden sense of a disturbing presence made Alice look up—to meet Harold Neale's eyes.

With a bow and a smile to her he went quickly across to Mrs. Neale, and exclaiming, " Well, dear mother, how goes it ? " kissed her tenderly.

Alice put down her book gently and had almost reached the door when Mrs. Neale cried :

"Do not run away, my dear. Let me at least introduce my son to you."

She was obliged to return and stood, with downcast eyes and crimson cheeks, unspeakably annoyed.

"I have already the pleasure of knowing Miss Ashland," said Harold, with a joyous ring in his tone, as he advanced to shake hands with her, and then stopped. Her attitude, her whole expression, showed she was not going to give him her hand, or to respond to his greeting beyond what civility required.

"How!—you know Miss Ashland?" asked his mother, greatly surprised. "Why did you not tell me so before?"

"Because, until your last letter you never mentioned the name of the young lady who has made your stay here so pleasant and profitable. I have to thank you heartily, Miss Ashland; but I fear you have forgotten me?"

"No," returned Alice, recovering herself, and remembering that it would not do to let her disappointment in him appear. "I was a little startled when you came in so unexpectedly."

"Then you had no idea he was my son?" asked Mrs. Neale.

"I thought it probable when you spoke of Peekskill, but—" She paused.

"No doubt you had many more interesting topics to discuss," said Harold, laughing. He wished to change the subject. He thought Alice's silence respecting himself arose from reluctance to · revert to the mortifying cir-

cumstances connected with their acquaintance-
ship.

"Good-evening," returned Alice, with a
pretty, slight, respectful courtesy to Mrs.
Neale. "I have put a mark in the book;
you can find the place easily. Good-evening,"
and, with a little hesitation, she gave her hand
to Harold.

"If you *will* go," he said, opening the door
for her. "I can see my mother is a different
creature and I am sure much of the improve-
ment is due to you."

Alice smiled, shook her head and escaped
downstairs; but not to the drawing-room; she
wanted to be alone. In their own apartment
the fire burned cheerfully and brightly,
and lighted the room sufficiently. Alice sat
down on the hearthrug and thought, in a hurried, confused way. "He has come—he is here,"
was the phrase that repeated itself over and
over again in her ears—the man who had
thought so lightly of her as to say he had better avoid her evident liking for him. Mrs. Craven was not honest, but she could not invent
such a story. Was it possible that that un-
affected, grave, composed man could be guilty
of such a piece of boyish coxcombry?

Guilty or not, she was almost dismayed to
feel so very, very glad to see him. She was
angry with herself; it wasn't want of proper
pride.

Then the past came back to her—oh, how
vividly!—all those months since their mem-
orable meeting at the great World's Fair!

At her first plunge in the brilliant life to which Mrs. Craven had introduced her, the only one whose presence gave her a sense of safety, of solid ground, was Harold Neale. But since they last met Alice had learned much; she had eaten of the fruit of the tree of knowledge and profited by the repast. She must not allow this consciousness of Harold's puerile vanity to disturb either her mind or her manners; she must be strong to live her own life, to mark out her own road. Mr. Neale could be nothing to her; she had much to see and to do apart from him. Indeed, she would resist these unprofitable musings now.

She rose as she came to this conclusion and looked round for her work-basket. She would take it to the drawing-room, and if Miss Miller, the locomotive, elderly young lady, was not playing the piano, she would ask her to go to the old Mission Church with her to-morrow. It was contemptible to sit and dream about follies.

The succeeding days, however, showed Alice that in the matter of avoiding Harold hers was not the only will at work.

He had evidently made up his mind to see as much as possible of her, and his mother seconded him in her gentle, kindly way. Mrs. Williams was soon won over completely.

She quite well remembered Harold once she saw him again, though when out of sight he slipped her memory.

To Alice, in spite of her resolutions to be coldly prudent and steadily distrustful, these days were unaccountably delightful. The hearty gratitude of Harold for her kind attentions to his mother touched her heart. His sincerity could not be doubted. A great longing to give him her whole confidence struggled within her against a stern determination to show no preference in her manner.

The weather was delightful and Harold often took his mother out driving. Alice was always asked to accompany them and sometimes accepted ; but Harold Neale could not resist the impression that she quietly avoided him. Was it that the associations connected with him were painful ? Could she class him with Nevin ? Did she think him a poltroon like his friend ? Or, had Mrs. Craven made mischief ? This was possible.

As Harold Neale pondered these things on his way back from a ramble along the beach, he caught sight of a certain brown hat and pheasant's breast which he knew well and soon overtook.

" Has Mrs. Williams a lazy fit that you are walking alone, Miss Ashland ? " he asked.

She looked up quickly, the color rising in her cheek for a moment. How well those delicate, flitting blushes became her !

" She is busy writing to her son," replied Alice. " My cousin, Mr. Ashland, has got him a good situation at Auckland, New Zealand, and dear Mrs. Williams is so glad."

" I suppose so," throwing away his cigar. " I did not know she had a son. You expect your cousin down here, do you not ? "

" We always expect him ; he is a little uncertain."

A pause. Neale was puzzled how to bring
the conversation round to herself and the
change he perceived in her manner.

"My mother is not quite so well to-day. I
persuaded her to stay indoors. Will you look
in on her when you go in ? You have done her
so much good ; you suit her exactly. In short,
if you do not think it audacious of me to mention such a possibility as your growing old, I
should say you will, in the course of inexorable
time, be just such an old lady as my mother
now is."

"That is a high compliment," said Alice,
with a pleased smile.

" Still it is difficult to fancy you anything but
young. Now do not turn toward the house.
It is so fresh and invigorating, though a little
wild ; the air will do you good and I want you
to explain something that puzzles me."

"What can it be ? " asked Alice. " I am not
likely to know more than you."

"You must not think me presumptuous; in
short, will you grant me plenary absolution for
anything I am going to say ? "

"Do not say anything disagreeable," said
Alice, looking up entreatingly.

"Do you think I would pain you in any
way? " asked Harold, meeting her eyes, the
expression in his own thrilling her with a
strange, wild delight that had in it something
of pain. "Well, I will trust to your understanding me," he resumed. " When I first

met you, Miss Ashland, we soon became friends; and I was under the impression that you felt how thoroughly I appreciated the frankness, the delightful sincerity of your nature; in short, that you were inclined to trust me, that you might, perhaps, if you needed it, have asked me to do you a service as naturally as you would an elder brother. Now, this is all changed. I cannot say where the change is, but **you** have closed your petals and hidden your heart. Tell me, has any one spoken against me to you? Why do you treat me as if I were more a stranger than the first day I met you?"

Alice was greatly puzzled how to answer. She could not repeat Mrs. Craven's speech respecting him; she could not otherwise account for the change in herself.

"No one has spoken against you, Mr. Neale," she said, keeping her eyes fixed on the ground. "I did not think I was so changed."

"Then you *are* changed?"

"I am very much changed—in every way. I feel so much older, so different. It seems years and years since I first met you. I do not intend to be—to be uncivil—"

"I want a great deal more than civility," said Harold, trying to steal a look into her eyes; "I want as much as I give, as I have given."

"It is growing very stormy," exclaimed Alice, abruptly, and, turning, she began to walk fast. Harold felt checked, but was not a man to be easily daunted.

"When I rushed off to see my mother," he resumed, "full of warmest gratitude to you for all your tender care of her, and looking forward to the pleasure of renewing our former friendship just at the same stage as we had been when separated by no fault of mine, I did not expect such a disappointment."

"I have read somewhere," said Alice, with a transparent attempt at evasion, "that nothing once broken off can ever be renewed again exactly as it was."

"I am sorry to hear you say so," said Harold, gravely. "I hoped earnestly that you would not think me less worthy of your frank friendliness *now* than you did four months ago. I can only accept your decision, feeling as poor Tom Moore must have done when he penned those exquisite lines in 'Lalla Rookh':

> "''Twas ever thus, from childhood's hour
> I've seen my fondest hopes decay,
> I never loved a tree or flower
> But 'twas the first to fade away.
> I never reared a dear gazelle
> To glad me with its bright blue eye,
> But when it came to know me well
> And love me, it was sure to die.'"

"You are very good. I do not wish to be rude or unkind," faltered Alice, deeply touched. Oh! ought she to have believed Mrs. Craven? Was it possible that he loved her, and she repelling him? Yet how could she explain?

"Rude or unkind," repeated Harold, "that you could never be. But I need not pain you by compelling you to speak more plainly. So good-by for the present. You will see my mother this evening, if you can?"

They had reached the gate. He opened it and raised his hat as she passed through. Then, setting it hard down, he turned and walked rapidly away in the teeth of the wind.

"Mr. Ashland arrived about half an hour ago, miss," said a servant whom she met in the hall.

Thankful for the timely notice, Alice slipped away to her own room to take off her hat, to think over the hopeless tangle in which she seemed involved.

As soon as she recovered herself she went into the little drawing-room to greet her cousin.

Mrs. Williams was sitting by the fire, knitting in hand, and a somewhat troubled expression on her countenance. Thomas Ashland was striding to and fro, his brow knit, his hands plunged in the side pockets of his coat.

"How do you do, Thomas?" said Alice, cheerfully. "I hope you are better?"

"No, I am not," roughly, stopping short in front of her; "and you are not well, either. You have been crying your eyes out. Don't deny it!—I see you have. What's the matter, little cousin? Can I help you?" These last words in a wonderfully softened tone that touched Alice.

"There is nothing the matter, Tom," she returned, stretching out her hands. "I have been walking against the wind, and it has made my eyes red and sore."

"Lies! lies!" muttered Ashland to himself.

"Where does that fellow Neale come from? How do you know him? I saw you walk past with him, and I watched and watched, and thought you'd never come back; but you did, still with him. How did you come to know him?"

"He is a friend of Mrs. Craven's," said Alice, dreadfully alarmed and much surprised.

"Ha! traitors every one. He is a traitor, too. You must speak to him no more, Alice; I forbid you."

"Cousin, I cannot be rude to an unoffending acquaintance because you bid me," returned Alice, firmly. "I do not particularly wish to walk or talk with Mr. Neale, but I will not be forbidden by you to speak to any one!"

"I suppose not! I am of no account in your eyes. I had better go. I am not wanted here."

"Oh, my gracious, Mr. Ashland!" cried Mrs. Williams.

"Really, Thomas, you are too silly," said Alice, with a pleasant laugh. "You must be hungry and out of temper to make a quarrel out of nothing. Don't you see how foolish it all is? Suppose I were to be angry with you if you walked out with—say Mrs. Jarrett, or even her daughter—"

Ashland interrupted her with a boisterous laugh.

"Just so. That *would* be a queer turn. Never mind, Alice; I wouldn't walk with a living soul if it would vex you."

"Well, do not vex me by being cross," she returned.

" All right ; I am a little out of sorts. Don't let us say anything more about it."

It had been a most trying day for Alice. She looked forward with infinite dread to dinner. She feared that her cousin might break out with some insulting speech to Harold. To her infinite relief, however, Harold Neale was not at table and the evening went over quietly.

" You are home early," said Mrs. Neale, when her son came to say good-night.

" And you are late ; I hardly expected you to be still up."

" I have been spending the evening with Mrs. Williams and Miss Ashland. She could not come to me because her cousin arrived to-day."

" Ah ! what is he like ? What do you think of him ? " asked Harold, eagerly.

" I cannot quite understand him ; I do not exactly like him. He was very silent at first this evening ; then he burst into talk, and talked well enough."

" Do you think he is more than a cousin to Miss Ashland ? Do you think she will marry him ? " asked Harold, slowly.

" It is impossible to say. I think not ; I hope not. I fancy she is a little afraid of him."

" I hope she is."

" Why, what has put such a wish into your head ? "

" Because—because I should like to marry her myself," returned Harold.

" Yes," said his mother, softly, " I have seen that you love her ; I wish that she may return your affection. She would be a sweet daughter to me. Do you think she likes you, Harold?"

"I cannot tell. I thought so last spring, but there was a rascally plot weaving round us at the time, and I was bound hand and foot. I will tell you all some day. Now I feel convinced some one has put her against me. She has changed; she distrusts me. Yet I have a sort of instinctive feeling that she might have loved me at one time." Harold passed his hand over his brow, but the mother's loving eyes caught an expression of pain.

"You love her very much, dear?" she asked, tenderly.

"With all my soul!" said Harold, emphatically. "But I have lost heart since she rebuffed me this morning. Still, I will hold on a while longer. I will see her and this cousin together, and judge for myself. If there is no hope I will be off home."

"I do not for a moment believe that you will find a rival in Mr. Ashland. I do not think Alice is even glad when he comes. She gives me, as I said, the impression of being afraid of him."

"Afraid? Oh, that can hardly be! Well, good-night. I fear I am not a lucky fellow, except in having such a dear old mother." He stooped, kissed her affectionately and went away to his room.

CHAPTER XIII.

AT dinner the next day Harold encountered Ashland. That eccentric person sat opposite to Harold and watched him all through dinner with a scowl of dislike, and, when by chance they spoke together, Ashland made a point of contradicting him on every point in the roughest and most abrupt manner. Harold bore all this with unshaken good - temper, occasionally sending a keen, inquiring glance across the table at his wordy *vis-a-vis*.

Dinner over, Mrs. Neale asked Alice and her friends to her room, and, though Ashland accepted, he did not stay long. With a confused apology about having promised some "fellows" to play a game of pool at the Monterey Hotel, he said good-night.

His parting glance made Alice uneasy.

It rested on Harold with so murderous an expression of hate and fury that she could not collect her thoughts for a few minutes. What danger did it threaten? or was her fancy grown morbid? She felt altogether unnerved and glad to retire, though there had been pleasant moments during the evening.

When Thomas Ashland next presented himself to his cousin he was in a very quiet, melancholy mood. He asked her to come out for a walk. The afternoon was soft and quiet, and Alice, glad to be able to grant a request of his, at once assented.

"We will go toward the old Mission," said

Ashland, as they passed through the gate. "There are not so many people that way."

"Very well," returned Alice, meekly.

"So that fellow Neale lives in the house," resumed Ashland. "I see him writing in his room."

"It is nice for him to be with his mother," said Alice, turning her eyes away.

"Very likely"—grimly. "Well, I'm not going to stay in the same house. I moved off to the hotel last night; didn't they tell you? No?"

"You would have been more comfortable here, would you not?"

To this Ashland made no reply, and they walked on in silence till they reached a shady nook. "Let us sit down," he said, abruptly. "It is not too cold for you, eh?"

"Oh, not at all," returned Alice, who was feeling uncomfortable.

"I said I would tell you my troubles when I came next, if you cared to listen," he began.

"Yes, I remember; and I shall be glad to hear them."

"It isn't a story to be glad about," said Ashland. "Well, here goes. I suppose now, Alice, you think I am a quiet, steady, stay-at-home man?"

"You always seem happy enough with us, and *we* are quiet, I am sure."

"Happy!—ay, that I am, if I could always be with you! Now I shall tell you what I really am—a desperate drunkard, nearly a hopeless one."

"That is impossible, Thomas!" cried Alice,

amazed. "Why, you rarely touch a glass of wine; you take only tea or milk or—"

"Ay, when I am with you. Don't you see, I dare not taste anything strong or I couldn't stop? Sometimes I keep clear of it for a month and begin to think I am cured ; then the dreadful, desperate longing for spirits, wine, anything, comes over me and I *must* have it, if I tore down walls and murdered men to get it!" He stopped and wiped his brow in great agitation. "When I first came over from New Zealand there was a good deal of excitement over both our affairs. I got better, calmer, stronger ; but after a bit the old craving came back. I have something more to say. Do you remember I once offered to marry you? I didn't care much about it, but I thought it might suit you at the time. Now I want you to marry me for *my* sake. Don't shrink away as if you feared me, Alice ; you *must* marry me. It drives me mad to see other people come near you, even women. I want you all to myself, away from every creature. That Neale dares to look at you and love you! I'd like to cut his throat! Answer me, Alice. Will you save me, and marry me?"

"I never dreamed you wished to marry me, Tom ; I have learned to think of you as a dear brother. I will do everything I can for you— *but* marry you, that I *cannot* do."

"What is your objection?"

"In truth, I have not the courage to—to marry you, after your account of your tendencies—your difficulties—"

"Then you are cold-hearted, indifferent." He burst into a mingled torrent of reproaches and entreaties. Alice, though trembling from head to foot, continued tenderly though firmly to refuse. At last, with a wild, despairing cry, he started up and rushed away toward the shore, and was soon out of sight.

Alice, though hardly able to stand, hastened in the opposite direction, growing calmer as she went, and at last reached the shelter of her own room, where she described to the astonished and sympathizing Mrs. Williams the trying interview she had just had.

"What will he do?" was Alice's cry. "He seemed quite out of his mind. I am afraid of his hurting himself."

"Oh, no, I don't suppose he will," returned Mrs. Williams, soothingly. "He is odd and eccentric, but I don't think he is so foolish as to do himself any harm. I will get Mrs. Jarrett to send over to the Monterey a little later on and find out if he has come in."

"It is all so unfortunate," said Alice. "Where can we turn? Mr. Bond seems to have quarreled with you, and Mr. Watts is so undecided, and now we have lost Thomas! I shall always be afraid of him, though I would give anything to be able to help him. Oh, how my head throbs!"

"Will you lie down? Perhaps you will get a little rest."

Mrs. Jarrett's messenger reported, first, that Mr. Ashland had gone out early and had not yet returned, and, on being again sent, brought word that Mr. Ashland had just come in and was in his room.

When Mrs. Jarrett's guests sat down to dinner Harold Neale was much exercised in his mind by the absence of Miss Ashland, especially as Mrs. Williams's honest face showed uneasiness and expectancy. She glanced at the door; she forgot to answer when spoken to; she scarcely ate. He remembered seeing Alice go with her cousin in the afternoon, and he drew the conclusion that they had come to some understanding—or misunderstanding.

"Mother, perhaps Miss Ashland will see you," he said in a low voice, as they rose from table.

She gave a little nod of assent, and went round to join Mrs. Williams at the door.

Harold saw them go out together, and went to his mother's room to await her return. Her visit seemed to him of portentous length, but she came at last. "Well?" he said, drawing her chair forward; "well?"

"She is better and only feared the heat and smell of dinner might bring back her headache; but, Harold, I think she has had a shock of some kind, she is so tremulous and shaken. I am sure the cousin has something to do with it, for Mrs. Williams said when we had left the room: 'If the poor dear had a father or a brother, or any one to look after her; I am no good.' I began to say something about her cousin, when she exclaimed: 'Don't talk of him; he frightens the life out of her.'"

"That is evident," cried Harold, much disturbed. "What is best to be done? I am so uncertain of her feelings toward me I fear to propose. As a rejected lover I should be no use whatever to her; as a friend I might be some help."

"Let us see what a few days may bring forth. I do not think she is averse to you."

Harold shook his head. "She never gives me the faintest encouragement. We are not even as good friends as we were at first. I wish her life were more fortunate."

"*You* will make it more fortunate yet, Harold," said Mrs. Neale, lovingly. "We know not what to-morrow may bring us."

The morrow brought a climax little anticipated.

Mrs. Williams had to post a parcel to her son that morning, a parcel she did not care to trust to any one's hands, but she lingered, loath to leave Alice in her nervous condition.

"I am too foolish," said Alice. "Go, dear, and mail your parcel; I will pay Mrs. Neale a visit while you're gone," and in a few minutes Mrs. Williams took her departure.

Alice was standing at a book-shelf, with her back to the open window which faced on to the conservatory, when the sound of a footfall made her turn round. To her dismay she saw Tom Ashland coming through the window.

"I frightened you yesterday; I know I did," said he. "I have been thinking a great deal since."

"Will you not sit down, Thomas?" said Alice, feeling that a crisis was at hand.

"No; there is no use in sitting down; I cannot rest. I must end all this. I shall never leave off drinking; I know it. I shall go down —down! Now, I am determined that shall never be. I was awfully tempted to finish Neale as I went by and saw him." A terrible, fierce, wild look came into his eyes. "But I had a duty to accomplish, and I resisted—I resisted! Alice, life is hard on us both. I will deliver us both. Look here!" He drew from his pocket a revolver, while Alice stood petrified with terror, yet keeping her wits about her, knowing that her first move meant death. "This will end all our troubles. You mustn't be frightened, my dear; it will not hurt you. I know the spot, and all I have to do is to touch the trigger and off you go; then I'll send a bullet through my own brain and join you. Don't look at the door. I'd be sorry to hurt you, but if you try to get away I will. I will never let you out of this alive."

"I am not going," said Alice, with marvelous, desperate self-control. "I think your plan is a good one, for life is so puzzling."

The unfortunate madman's countenance relaxed. "Ah, that is right. You are true after all; come!"

"One thing, however, I must do before—before we die. I promised Father Ignatius of the Mission to bring over the picture of the infant St. John this morning. You or I must take it, for I cannot break my word at such a time."

"Ah, perhaps; yes, you ought not. Well, get the picture and I will wait till you return. Don't be long, for I'm anxious we should be off."

Alice opened the door, went out, and then fled wildly along the veranda—not into the house, not to call assistance, but to Harold Neale's room. She felt sure that Ashland would rush to wreak vengeance either on her or his supposed rival.

Harold was writing, as he often did, at a table beside the window, which was open. He was resting his head on his hands, thinking over his mother's advice and balancing the pros and cons, when Alice, white as death, her eyes wild with terror, flew into the room.

Harold started up, his first idea being that she was making her escape from danger or pursuit; but before he could speak she began in frantic haste to close the window, then the shutters, while she kept repeating: "Lock the door—bolt it! Oh, do—do lock it!"

"What is the matter, for Heaven's sake?" cried Harold. "My dear Miss Ashland, you are safe with me."

"No—no! I want to save you! He will murder you! Oh, come back into the corner! Do not hold me; I must fasten the door!" Then, leaning back against it exhausted, she went on: "He is mad—quite mad, Thomas is. He wanted to murder me; he was very near murdering you. He will come now; he has a horrible revolver."

Here a step was heard in the passage. Quite beside herself with fear, Alice darted to Harold and threw her arms around him.

"He is coming—he is coming!" she whispered, as she clung to him.

"Dearest," said Harold, straining her to his heart, "you will be ill. Let me take you to my mother. If your cousin is mad, he must be prevented from doing mischief to himself or others. You are trembling—you can hardly stand," and he tried to lift her, but she evaded him.

"I will not let you go," she said, faintly. "He will murder you. I will not let you go."

"Ashland is not coming here," said Harold ; "he would have been here before. Let me take you away; I must know what is going on." Still supporting her, he opened the door. All was quiet, but a distant buzz of talk came from the hall.

"You must come upstairs. You shall be safe with my mother. I will see to it."

Half leading, half carrying her, Harold took Alice with infinite care to his mother.

"She has had an awful fright," he said; "get her some wine. I scarcely know what is the matter, but don't leave her. I shall return when I find Mrs. Williams."

"My dear child, you are more dead than alive," cried Mrs. Neale. "Put her on the lounge, Harold."

Alice could not speak. She tried still to hold Neale, but he, gently kissing her hand, disengaged himself and hurried away.

In the hall he found Mrs. Jarrett and all the servants talking eagerly. "Oh, Mr. Neale!" said the lady of the house, "we are all so frightened. Jim here—the stable-boy—about ten minutes ago saw Mr. Ashland without his hat, and a great pistol in his hand, tearing across the lawn as hard as he could, and looking quite wild."

"Indeed!" cried Harold. "What direction did he take?"

"He turned right, and ran straight toward the beach," said the boy. "He seemed to come from Miss Ashland's room."

"Heavens! I hope he hasn't hurt the dear young lady," cried Mrs. Jarrett, fussing away in the direction of her room.

"My mother has Miss Ashland quite safe," said Harold, reaching his hat and going out to see what had become of the madman.

When Mrs. Williams returned she found everything topsy-turvy, and when she heard of Ashland's mad act her dismay can be imagined. It was some little time before Alice could speak calmly to Harold. She felt certain that in her intense excitement she had betrayed herself.

"How is my poor cousin?" she said to Mrs. Neale, who was sitting with her.

"My dear, I'm afraid his is a hopeless case. He was last seen tearing toward the pier, and "—but looking toward the door—"here is Harold."

As she spoke Harold Neale entered the room. It was a moment of profound embarrassment.

"I am sorry to see that you have not quite recovered the dreadful shock you have sustained; and you must brace yourself for another."

"What do you mean?" cried Alice.

"Your cousin, poor fellow, I'm heartily sorry for him; but perhaps it is for the best. Mine is an ungrateful task, but you had better hear it from one who loves you than from a stranger. Your cousin, after leaving your room, rushed down to the beach, revolver in hand. Several men tried to capture him, but he flourished his weapon and fled. On reaching the beach he mounted the pier, where the fishing boats are, and ran along it. When he reached the end of it he turned for a moment, placed the pistol to his head, fired and fell backward into the water. The fishermen recovered the body and an inquest will be held."

There was a long silence.

"Heaven have mercy on him!" sighed Alice, at last, resuming her seat on the lounge. "But it will be long before I can forget this dreadful day. Poor Cousin Thomas! my heart aches for him; but better dead than mad."

"Yes, poor fellow!" said Harold. "But I want to speak of something else, even at this awful time—something which concerns the future of my life. You know what it is. I have longed for weary months to say: 'Alice, I love you.' I almost despaired, when something in your fears for me to-day—something in the clasp of your arms—gave me a faint hope."

He paused, and Alice, half charmed, half frightened, made a little hesitating movement, as if to give him her hand, and then drew back.

'Ah, you distrust me,' cried Harold.
"Why? Do be candid with me. Do not keep
me in the torture of suspense.'

'I have been vexed with you," began Alice,
with natural sweet frankness, "and I am almost ashamed to say why. But I will tell you.
When you went home to Peekskill from Chicago I was sorry. You always seemed
true and earnest—a real friend—and I said I
was sorry. Then Mrs. Craven told me you are
pleased to go because—because you thought I
was in love with you and showed it too much."

"It was an infernal lie," cried Harold, with
more energy than politeness, "invented by an
unscrupulous woman! Look in my eyes, Alice,
and tell me whom you believe—Mrs. Craven or
me? I am incapable of making such a speech
about any woman."

She raised her eyes to his; then a soft, shy
smile broke over her face and she said, very
low and steadily:

"I believe you."

"Then one difficulty is removed. Alice, I
have loved you almost from the beginning of
our acquaintance; can you give me a little in
return?"

He held out his hand and Alice put hers
into it.

"Dearest," he exclaimed, "put your arms
around me and say : 'Harold, I love you.'"
He raised her arms to his neck and clasped
her to his heart with passionate force. "Whisper it to me and I will be satisfied."

But a long, soft kiss stopped further ut-

terance ; past, present and future all merged in
that intense moment.

Mrs. Craven was seated in the drawing-room
of her Twenty-first Street mansion, New York,
reading the latest society novel, when her husband, the gallant major, entered somewhat abruptly. "Well, Mary, my dear, I told you and
that fool of a brother of yours that it was an
evil day for him, though a day of blessing for
her, when he broke off his engagement to Alice
Ashland."

"Why, my dear husband, you couldn't expect poor Wilfred to marry on nothing."

"Poor Wilfred—bah ! With all respect to
you, my love, all my sympathies were with
Miss Ashland, and I think Heaven itself must
have interfered to save her 'from a fellow content to live off the crumbs that fall from my
table. Read that." He thrust a newspaper
into her hand ; it was the latest San Francisco
Examiner.

The leading page had a column headed with
the startling headlines :

"Suicide of a Millionaire.—Mr. Thomas Ash-
land Suicides at Monterey after Attempting the
Life of His Cousin.—Sensational Scenes at the
Mission House," etc., etc.

The article then went on to detail with the
minuteness which has made the *Examiner*
famous on the Pacific Slope the account of the
tragedy with which the reader is acquainted,
and closed with stating : "It is rumored that
Miss Ashland, who inherits his vast estate, will

shortly, billed to the altarly Mr. Harold Neale
of Peekskill-on-the Hudson who first became
acquainted with the heiress a few months ago
at the World's Fair."

Mrs. Craven had read the article through in
an unconcerned manner until she came to the
concluding passage. The writing on the wall
of Belshazzar's palace could scarcely have filled
those who saw it with deeper emotion than
that which the sight of those lines evoked in
their reader, but the meaning in her case had
nothing of mystery in it; it was the very plain-
ness that drove the color from her cheek and
turned her heart to stone.

"Well," said the major, "I'm very glad
that Harold Neale carried off the prize, for he
is a man, every inch of him."

Wealth has not led Mr. and Mrs. Harold
Neale to forsake the clearer spring of their
quiet home on the Hudson for the troubled
waters of a swim society existence among the
McAllisters of city life. Peace and happiness
reign supreme in the picturesque home near
the glens and hills that Rip Van Winkle caused
to echo with his laugh, and of Ala and Harold the poet might have truly said

> Along the cool sequestered vale of life
> They keep the even tenor of their way.

THE END.